# The Hidden Boy

# JON BERKELEY

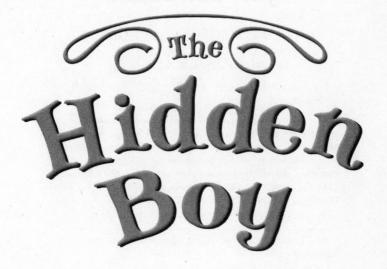

The Hidden Boy

KATHERINE TEGEN BOOKS
*An Imprint of HarperCollins Publishers*

Katherine Tegen Books
is an imprint of HarperCollins Publishers.

The Hidden Boy
Text copyright © 2010 by Jon Berkeley
Illustrations copyright © 2010 by Brandon Dorman

Library of Congress Cataloging-in-Publication Data
Berkeley, Jon.
The hidden boy / Jon Berkeley. — 1st ed.
        p.    cm.
Summary: When Bea and her family are transported aboard an
underwater bus to a strange land, her younger brother Theo is lost
during the voyage, and somehow it falls to Bea to find out what has
become of him.
ISBN 978-0-06-168758-7
[1. Adventure and adventurers—Fiction. 2. Missing
children—Fiction. 3. Brothers and sisters—Fiction.] I. Title.
II. Title: Hidden boy.
PZ7.B45255Hi   2010                      2009012272
[Fic]—dc22                                    CIP
                                               AC

Typography by Andrea Vandergrift
10  11  12  13  14   LP/RRDB   10  9  8  7  6  5  4  3  2  1
❖
First Edition

*Here's to Ray,*
*Who left unexpectedly*
*Having exceeded his brief as a human being*
*by a substantial margin.*

# Contents

# Bontoc

When Bea Flint opened the front door, just a few days before her little brother imploded, she found a stocky man in a sea captain's uniform waiting on the doormat. His cheeks were flamingo pink, and a gray beard fringed his chin. He stuck out his hand abruptly and smiled.

"Captain Bontoc," he said. He looked as if he had just stepped off a packet of frozen cod.

"Oh," said Bea. She could not remember hearing the doorbell ring, but she supposed it must have. She kept her hands by her sides. "Are you looking for someone?" she said.

"Aye," said Captain Bontoc. "I'm looking for a Mrs. Flint. Or possibly a Mr. Flint."

"We have one of each," said Bea. "Which would you prefer?"

The captain looked slightly sheepish. "Not absolutely sure, missy. Somebody named Flint bought a raffle ticket in aid of the Salty Dogs Retirement Fund, but the ticket got a bit wet, so it's hard to read. I'm here to deliver the prize."

"What did we win?" asked Ma from over Bea's shoulder.

"You'll be Mrs. Flint," said Captain Bontoc, removing his cap. He held out the ticket stub. "The name's a bit blurred, but you can still make out the address. Somebody here is the lucky winner of a Blue Moon Once-in-a-Lifetime Adventure Holiday."

Ma turned the ticket over in her tattooed hands. "I don't remember buying this," she said.

"Maybe Pa bought it," said Bea.

"Never mind who bought it," said Granny Delphine from the narrow hallway. There were six people living in the Flints' cramped apartment, and a crowd could develop quickly. Granny Delphine had round glasses that gave her the look of an owl in search of its supper. "Let's have the details, if you please, young man," she said.

"Right away," said the captain hastily, and he produced a small brochure from an inside pocket. "You'll find it all in here," he said. "The tour leaves from the

Blue Moon office on Wednesday at eleven P.M. sharp. Groups of seven only. No pets, nontransferable, no cash prizes."

"How long is the holiday?" asked Ma, taking the brochure from the captain.

"All the details are in the brochure," said Captain Bontoc. "It'll be the trip of a lifetime!" He replaced his hat and backed toward the stairs. "I must be off, if you'll excuse me. Got some caulking to do."

In the days that followed Captain Bontoc's unexpected visit, the brochure he had left seemed to travel around the apartment of its own accord. One day it would be wedged between the damp-wrinkled magazines in the bathroom, the next day perched on the edge of the kitchen table waiting to be swept off as someone squeezed past. Everyone in the Flint family read it at least twice, except Theo. He just looked at the pictures.

The brochure came to rest beside Granny Delphine as she dozed in her armchair on the evening of their departure. Bea was searching for her binoculars when she spotted it, and for what must have been the tenth time she picked it up and looked closely at the picture on the cover. The words BLUE MOON ONCE-IN-A-LIFETIME ADVENTURE HOLIDAYS curled across the sky in large yellow letters, and the closer you looked at it the more adventure you could see. In the foreground was a tree with many trunks and broad branches radiating outward like spokes. *A banyan tree*, said Bea to herself. She was more often to be found reading encyclopedias than anything else, and she knew about such things.

There was a platform built in the tree, and a tent pitched on the platform, and a large family who appeared to be having the best time you could possibly have in a tree, or anywhere else for that matter. They were swinging from ropes, they were picking enormous fruit, they were sliding down the sloping roots and calling to one another with their hands cupped around their mouths, the way people do only in pictures. A woman in a safari suit busied herself at a cooking fire, smiling like a dentist's assistant. A saucer-eyed monkey peeped from between the banyan leaves, and a striped snout could just be seen in the shadows among the roots. Tall mountains stood like crooked pegs in the distance.

Bea's eyes returned to the base of the tree. There was not much she didn't know about animals, yet the creature snuffling among the tree roots was strangely unfamiliar. It looked like a miniature pig with zebra stripes, except that zebra stripes were seldom bright green, as these were. The details were frustratingly small. Bea glanced at her sleeping grandmother, then at the old lady's round spectacles, resting next to her knotted hand on the arm of the chair. Bea hesitated for a moment, then picked them up and placed them quickly on her nose.

The springy wire arms of the glasses curled around her ears like live things, and she sat back on her heels, startled. The picture on the brochure seemed to leap toward her. She could see now that it was swarming with life. There was an animal behind almost every leaf on the tree, and the air hummed with fat honeybees. The smoke from the campfire billowed into the sky, and in the far distance great birds hovered over the mountains.

Something was missing from the picture too, but it took her a moment to realize what it was. The small boy who had been swinging from the branches when she first examined it was nowhere to be seen. Bea turned the brochure over, thinking that she must have seen him on the back cover, but he was not there, either.

A muffled snort made her look up quickly at her grandmother. Granny Delphine herself appeared different through the glasses. Her expression was sharper, and her nose curved like a beak. A network of wrinkles traced the contours of her face like a minutely detailed map. Bea was overtaken by a panicky feeling that she was seeing more than she was meant to. She tried to unhook the glasses from her ears, but their curling arms had tangled themselves in her hair. Granny Delphine was rubbing her eyes with her fingertips. Bea managed to free the spectacles just in time, replacing them on the arm of the chair as the old lady opened her eyes.

"I was . . . just looking at the brochure," said Bea quickly.

"I didn't ask what you were doing, child," said Granny Delphine. She gave Bea a suspicious look. "Why don't you go and help your mother?"

Bea got up and hurried into the kitchen, where her mother was rummaging through the drawers, looking for plastic cutlery.

Ma glanced at the brochure that Bea still clutched in her hand. "I still think there could be more information," she said with a frown.

"There's enough," said Bea, a little too quickly. "It wouldn't be an adventure if we knew what to expect, would it?"

Ma took the brochure. "'Strictly groups of seven.

No pets,'" she read again. "Why seven?"

"I'm bringing Nails," said Theo from the corner.

"You can't bring Nails," said Ma. "It says *no pets*."

"We need seven people," said Theo, "and we only have six." His voice whistled through the gap where his two front teeth had been.

"Nails is a meerkat," said Ma. "Meerkats aren't people."

"Mine is," said Theo. A stubborn look came over his face, and he disappeared into his bedroom.

Granny Delphine appeared at the door of the kitchen. "What's the holdup?" she said, and everyone jumped slightly and tried to look busy. "It's quarter to ten," said Granny Delphine, who never wore a watch but always knew the time. Her glasses had returned to their familiar perch on her nose, and her magnified eyes swept the room like spotlights. "The tour leaves at eleven, and if the brochure says we need seven people then we need seven people."

"I'm sure they'll take six of us," said Ma.

"I'm sure they won't," said Granny Delphine.

"Anyway, we *are* seven," said Bea, "if you count Phoebe."

"So we are," said Granny Delphine. "Run next door

and get her; there's a good girl. Tell her we're leaving in ten minutes."

"We can't bring the neighbors' daughter just to make up the *numbers*," said Ma, as the door slammed after Bea.

Granny Delphine fixed Ma with a hard stare. "That child's parents have been playing poker for eleven straight days," she said. "They've lost their car, their couch and their cat. What do you think they'll bet next?"

Ma looked at Granny Delphine with a shocked expression. "They wouldn't!" she said.

"They can't if she comes with us," said Granny Delphine. She folded her arms crisply to close the subject. "Is the van packed?" she said.

The van was not packed, but once Granny Delphine had asked the question it almost packed itself. Pa thundered down the wooden stairs two at a time, a suitcase over each shoulder. Bea, who always packed days in advance, disappeared into Theo's room to make sure he had everything he needed in his backpack. Gabby ticktocked into the kitchen and began making a skyscraper of sandwiches from everything that remained in the fridge, including the frost.

Gabby was thin and unsmiling, with short red hair

that never seemed to grow. She had been in the apartment when they moved in, and since she had nowhere else to go she had never left. She moved like a clockwork toy, and she never uttered a word. Between her shoulder blades she had an imaginary key, which needed winding twice a day or she would come to a complete standstill.

Before ten minutes had passed, Granny Delphine was trotting down the stairs like a silver-haired sheepdog, driving the stragglers before her. She carried a small crocodile-skin case inscribed with her name in silver letters: MRS. D. WALKER. The family Flint emerged onto the pavement under a darkening sky and began to jigsaw themselves into the van wherever they could find space among the cases and bags.

Picture for a moment the passenger list of that rust-spotted vehicle. There was Pa, also known as Bald Mountain, wedged into the driver's seat and drumming his fingers on the wheel. Beside him sat Theo, as small as Pa was big, holding on his knee an army camouflage backpack that twitched suspiciously. Next to him was Ma, who was trying to remember what she had forgotten to pack. In the middle row Granny Delphine sat like an alert owl, and Gabby wrote in a small green

notebook with a silver pen, her elbow resting on a pile
of sandwiches. In the back of the van Bea settled herself
among the sleeping bags while they waited for Phoebe
to appear. She wondered what the wilderness would be
like. She pictured herself surrounded by teeming wild-
life with no fear of mankind, like the picture on the
brochure.

"Did you bring the map?" asked Ma.

"No need," said Bald Mountain. "The bus leaves
from the Blue Moon office on the canal docks. I know
those docks like the back of my hand."

Theo looked at the back of Pa's hand and wondered
what he meant. It was decorated with a tattoo that Ma
had put there before even Bea was born, when Pa still
rode with the Flying Rascals Motorcycle Club and Ma
was the busiest tattoo artist in town. The tattoo showed
a burning bridge with curling tongues of flame that
licked around Pa's wrist. It did not look like a map of
any kind to Theo.

In the back of the van Bea was also thinking of that
tattoo. The thought of the burning bridge gave her a
sudden queasy feeling as she squirmed among the sleeping bags. She remembered how strange the picture on
the brochure had looked through Granny Delphine's

spectacles, and pushed down a guilty feeling that was rising in her chest.

And Phoebe Lu, the neighbors' daughter? She took the last six stairs at a flying leap, touching down briefly on the doorstep before launching herself out of the door like a kangaroo. She had short black hair, and one brown arm and one white one, having just had her plaster cast removed. She was fearless and thin, and she would have been even thinner if she had not eaten dinner with the Flint family every day, as her parents were far too caught up in the flip of a card or the tumble of dice to worry about feeding their daughter.

"In the back, Phoebe, quickly," called Granny Delphine, "and pull the door after you. There's no time to lose." The clouds broke as the van pulled away from the curb, and a warm rain began to fall. Granny Delphine stared straight ahead, not wanting to take a last look at the apartment. She knew she would probably never see it again, and she was afraid someone would spot the tears in her eyes.

# Late

**S**hortly after the Flint family had left their apartment for the canal docks, two cars appeared from the other end of the street and drove at breakneck speed along the wet road. You could tell at once they were Gummint cars. They were painted gray with pink doors, and each one contained four men. They pulled up at the door of the apartment building and their hand brakes went *skrunk* in unison. Their occupants piled out and hurried up the wooden stairs in single file. They crowded onto the landing outside the Flints' door without a word. One of them, a man with dark glasses and a small, prim mouth, reached out and knocked sharply on the door.

The Gummint men waited for a reply, eight of them in suits and ties, sweating in the heat of the summer rainstorm. The man with the dark glasses checked the address in a small notebook and looked up again at the silent door. He pursed his lips. "They've gone," he said. He stepped to one side, and another man took out a fat pistol and aimed it at the lock. There was a loud bang and a puff of smoke, and the splintered door swung slowly open.

The men swarmed into the apartment and began to take it apart like ants dismantling a cockroach. They upended drawers and ransacked cupboards and frowned into the empty fridge. They scattered books and rummaged through magazines. They emptied all the wardrobes except for Theo's, which featured toxic-sock defenses that even their crack search methods could not overcome. They beheaded the flowers and shredded the curtains and disemboweled the sofa. They shattered the lightbulbs and tore up the floorboards and punched pictures from their frames, but whatever they were looking for was nowhere to be found. They emerged disgruntled onto the landing, with sweat-stained armpits and pillow feathers pasted to their greasy foreheads.

A woman waited for them outside the next-door apartment, wearing a housecoat and pink bedroom slippers. She had straggly blond hair and bags under her eyes. "Are you from the Gummint?" she asked, as though they could have been anyone else.

"Maybe," said the man with the dark glasses.

"They've taken my daughter, Phoebe." The woman sniffed loudly. "You'd better get after them, as soon as you've given us the reward money."

Dark Glasses consulted his notebook. "Mr. Lu?" he said.

"He's my husband," said the woman.

"He left it a bit late to call us," said Dark Glasses. "I'm afraid you might never see your daughter again."

Mrs. Lu's eyes opened wide and she blew out a jet of smoke. "What do you mean, *never*?" she said. "It's your job to track them down, isn't it?"

"Rest assured that we'll do everything we can," said the Gummint man, putting away his notebook.

"Would," muttered the man with the pistol.

"That's right," said Dark Glasses. "We would do everything we could, assuming we were from the Gummint."

"Which we may or may not be," added the other man, adjusting his tie.

"And the reward?" said Mrs. Lu. She stubbed out

her cigarette on the doorjamb.

"You'll get that through the usual channels," said the Gummint man.

Mrs. Lu glanced back into the gloom of her apartment, where half a dozen players sat around a card table, belching smoke and stacking their chips. "But we need it *now*!" she said.

Dark Glasses shook his head. "Takes six to eight weeks, I'm afraid."

The woman's shoulders slumped and she turned to go back inside. There was a pizza crust stuck to her backside. Before she closed the door she hesitated, and turned back to the Gummint men. "Would any of you men like to buy a stove?" she said.

# Gone

The Flint family's van rattled its way along the docks, following the glint of the rails that were set into the cobbles. The rain had dwindled to nothing and the sky was turning a deep indigo. Phoebe, who had a fascination with anagrams and could produce them with bewildering speed, was reeling off anagrams of Bea's name. "Fable tin." She laughed. "Bean lift. Final bet." She stopped after this last one, and her face grew thoughtful.

"Did you ask your mother to feed Theo's meerkat, Phoebe?" called Ma.

"Mm-hmm," said Phoebe.

"She'll feed it to her dog," muttered Pa.

"I left out enough food to last him a couple of days anyway," said Ma, unaware that at that very moment a

Gummint man with a surgical glove was rummaging for clues in the meerkat's bowl.

"Nails will be fine," said Bea. Theo smiled to himself and clutched his backpack a little tighter.

Granny Delphine looked at the back of the boy's head and sighed. "Either way, it's all the same," she said under her breath, though no one would have known what she meant even if they could have heard her.

"This is it," said Pa. "Clipper Quay. Look out for number eleven."

They slowed to a crawl, searching for numbers on the unlit warehouses. They found number ten and number twelve. Sandwiched between them was a car wash, standing like a mechanical mammoth against the evening sky. There was a small booth to one side, lit with a greenish fluorescent light. A neon sign read, MR. WAXY. Pa frowned. "That can't be right," he said.

"Did you check the back of your hand?" asked Bea.

"Very funny," said Pa.

The door of the booth opened suddenly, and Captain Bontoc popped out as though he had been stored under pressure. He marched quickly toward them. "Ahoy, there!" he said. "Not a moment too soon. Let's get you signed up and your luggage loaded. Look lively!" He glanced at the sky. "Departure in ten minutes."

"I have some questions," said Ma, leaning out of her window.

"All in good time, ma'am," said Captain Bontoc. "If you'd just line up for check-in I'll transfer your baggage to the bus; then we'll fill you in on the details."

"What bus?" asked Phoebe as they climbed out of the van.

Captain Bontoc had already grabbed several suitcases and wedged a couple of sleeping bags under his arms, so he pointed with his beard. In the shadows behind the booth stood a battered bus with a rather strange shape. It seemed to be cobbled together from several vehicles, and the underside was curved like the hull of a submarine. Six wheels poked out through open hatches in the hull like cannon from a sailing ship. Along the side were stenciled the words:

SKY BLACK, MOON BLUE
NINE SOULS GO THROUGH.

"It's a busmarine!" said Theo.

"That's the Blue Moon Mobile," said Captain Bontoc. "One of only two in existence."

Pa examined the vehicle in fascination. "What does she run on?" he asked.

"Water and land," grunted Captain Bontoc. "She's just as happy either way."

"That's not what I meant—," said Pa.

Granny Delphine interrupted him. "There's no time for chitchat. Get yourselves checked in, or we'll miss the tour altogether."

They queued up outside the booth. It seemed a strange start to a holiday, but Granny Delphine was not in a mood for argument, and it was a foolish person who would try. From the end of the queue Bea stood on tiptoe to see in through the window. There was a desk inside the booth, and behind it a back door fitted with a turnstile. A man with cropped gray hair like a scrubbing brush sat behind the desk. He was examining a complicated chart that was spread out in front of him, and he glanced up as Pa squeezed in through the door.

"Name?" said the man.

"Herbie Flint," said Pa. "Bald Mountain to my friends."

The man wrote something on his chart. He did not seem too concerned with what Pa's friends might call him. "Through the turnstile and board the bus, please," he said without looking up again. "Next!"

"Mrs. Delphine Walker," said Granny Delphine, and marched through the turnstile without waiting to be told.

One by one they entered the booth, and the brush-haired man gave each of them a brief but searching look before making notes on the chart and sending them through the turnstile. He seemed to want to get through them as quickly as possible, but when Clockwork Gabby ticked into the booth he straightened up and looked at her wordlessly for a moment.

"Your name?" he said eventually.

"It's Gabby," called Bea through the door.

The man bent over his chart and made a number of notations. "Surname?" he said.

"Clockwork," said Theo, who stood behind Gabby. He was clutching his backpack to his chest, and his hair stood up on one side where he had fallen asleep against Ma's arm in the van.

"No, it's not," said Bea to the man. "She lives with us. You can just put Flint."

Bea stepped into the booth and looked curiously at the chart that was spread out on the desk. It seemed to be based on the solar system, but the planets and their moons were overlaid with such a complex network of lines, trajectories, notes and symbols that it was hard to imagine how any sense could be made of it. It was weighted down at one corner by a thick glass jar with a screw top. The pencil with which the man was making notes on the chart was sharpened to a pinpoint, and his writing was microscopic.

"Name?" said the man, looking up.

"Bea Flint," said Bea. She craned her neck to try to see what he was writing. "That's an interesting map," she said.

The man found a tiny space on the chart and filled it in with his pinpoint pencil.

"Are we going to another planet?" asked Bea.

The brush-haired man looked up and smiled. "In a bus?" he said. "I hardly think so."

"It's not exactly a normal bus," said Bea.

"It's amphibious," said the man, "but I've never known it to fly." He glanced out through the window of the booth. A fat yellow moon hung in the night sky. It seemed to be fringed on one side with a hint of blue. "Your bus is about to leave," he said. "You'd better hurry."

Captain Bontoc bustled in, dusting his hands. "All bags loaded," he said. "Is she the last?"

"She's the last," said the brush-haired man.

The captain placed his hand on Bea's back and propelled her gently but firmly through the turnstile. She found herself facing the open hatch in the side of the Blue Moon Mobile, and she took a deep breath and climbed aboard. As she did so she heard the brush-haired man speak to the captain. "Good luck," he said; then a moment later she heard him call out something that sounded like, "You're forgetting the Squeak Jar, Bontoc."

The inside of the Blue Moon Mobile was as haphazard as the outside. The captain's seat was a barber's swivel chair, and the passenger seats seemed to have been salvaged from at least three different vehicles. At the back of the busmarine there was a large contraption of red and chrome with a sign on it saying, ICE CREAM. Theo was rattling the handle of the ice-cream machine. "It's not working," he said to Bea. "I pressed the button lots of times, and I pulled the lever. The machine just said, 'Ouch,' but no ice cream came out."

"Machines can't talk. Not ice-cream machines, anyway."

"This one did," said Theo.

Captain Bontoc climbed into the driver's chair, and the hatches closed with a thump and a hiss. He placed the glass jar from the booth on the dashboard and unscrewed the lid; then he swiveled quickly to face the passengers. "Take your seats, please, ladies and gents," he bellowed. "Remain seated while the Blue Moon Mobile is in motion, and use the belts provided. No eating, drinking or smoking, and"—he paused as he surveyed the passengers—"definitely no sleeping."

Theo sat down in the backseat and folded his arms. Bea helped him with his seat belt before sliding in past Phoebe on the bench in front of him. The captain spun his chair back to face the controls and started the engine. It made a sound like a dozen fat motorcycles in convoy, which brought a smile to Pa's face. The Blue Moon Mobile pulled out of its parking bay, but instead of turning toward the dockside it swung around and crawled slowly into the car wash. Captain Bontoc began to crank energetically a handle that protruded from the side of his chair, and the sights of a periscope descended slowly from the ceiling above him. At the same time Bea felt a grinding motion beneath her feet, and she looked out of the window to see a broad fin extending from the hull below her. It seemed like a lot of preparation just to go through a car wash.

The captain honked the horn twice, and the car wash jerked to life. The massive brushes advanced toward them like columns of spinning seaweed, spattering the windshield with foam.

"If you look at the sky to your right," shouted Captain Bontoc, "you'll observe something you don't see very often." He gestured toward the busmarine windows without taking his eyes off the approaching brushes.

Phoebe leaned out across the aisle to get a better look. "The moon is blue!" she said.

"So it is," said Ma. "Look at that, Theo!" she called over her shoulder.

Theo said nothing.

*He's sulking about the ice-cream machine*, thought Bea.

Within seconds the view was obscured by the car wash, which enveloped the Blue Moon Mobile like a shaggy storm. It was the roughest car wash that anyone on board could remember. The huge brushes roared against the busmarine's skin, and water surged around them until it felt as though they were totally submerged. Clockwork Gabby gripped the seat in front until her knuckles went white, and Granny Delphine laid her hand gently on Gabby's wrist. Excitement shone in Phoebe's eyes, and she fumbled with the buckle on her seat belt until she was stopped by a roar from Captain Bontoc.

"Leave it be, missy!" he bellowed, without looking around. He was wrestling with the enormous steering wheel now, his face pressed to the eyepiece of the peri-scope. There was a plunging sensation, and the Blue Moon Mobile was unmistakably underwater. The brushes looked more like weeds with every passing second, and they thrashed about in the murky water like trees in a storm.

"I don't like this," said Ma, and Bald Mountain put his huge tattooed arm around her.

"Hold on tight!" shouted Captain Bontoc. The Blue Moon Mobile tilted sharply to starboard before right-ing itself. Bubbles swirled around them, and suddenly Bea spotted the strangest thing of all. Ahead of them there was another busmarine in the seething water. It appeared to be heading straight toward them, push-ing through the weeds at full speed. The lights were on inside, and as it approached she could see that it was empty except for its captain, a jug-eared man with a walrus mustache. He was dressed in the same uniform as Captain Bontoc, and he raised his peaked cap in salute.

Captain Bontoc took his eyes from the periscope for a moment. He raised his own cap briefly to his opposite number before grabbing the wildly spinning steering wheel and returning his attention to the periscope. The other busmarine was so close now that Bea was sure their fins would scrape together. There was a loud and rather unexpected sound, a sort of *sssssnup!*, like an inside-out pop. Something about it made her distinctly uneasy. It was not the kind of sound she thought an underwater collision would make, but she held her breath anyway and hoped there would be no damage.

In the driver's seat Captain Bontoc reached out and, without taking his eyes from the periscope, clapped the lid onto the Squeak Jar and screwed it tight.

"Did you *see* that?" said Phoebe, her mouth open in astonishment as she stared after the retreating vehicle. Bea just nodded.

"Where exactly are we?" demanded Ma in a loud voice.

"We're almost there, ma'am," answered the captain. Sure enough, the water around them was getting calmer, and there was a series of thumps as the wheels made contact with solid ground. The Blue Moon Mobile began to climb a bumpy slope, and before long they emerged from the water, which streamed from the windows to reveal a landscape quite unlike the grimy warehouses of the canal docks. To their right a tangled forest spread out into the distance, and beyond it they could see tall mountains like the ones in the brochure, lit by a moon as blue as a jay.

The Blue Moon Mobile rumbled to a halt and Captain Bontoc killed the engine. Inside the busmarine there was silence as everyone tried to take in what had just happened. Ma removed Pa's arm gently from around her shoulders, and the color returned to Gabby's knuckles. Phoebe unbuckled her seat belt and hurled herself into the empty seat opposite, pressing her face against the window. Bea stared out at the forest that began a stone's throw from the busmarine, and for once even Granny Delphine seemed lost for words.

"How *about* that!" said Pa. He ran his hand over his shiny scalp and turned around with a grin. "What did you think of that, Theo?"

There was no answer from the backseat. Bea scrambled to her knees and looked over the back of her bench.

There was no sign of Theo at all. On the seat where he had been sitting there was nothing but an army backpack and a slowly disappearing dent in the upholstery beneath a still-fastened seat belt.

Bea's eyes opened wide, and her insides turned to cold jelly. She remembered the sucking pop she had heard as they passed the other Blue Moon Mobile in the turbulent water. Too late she realized that it had come from directly behind her, right where Theo had been. She got down quickly from her seat and looked under the benches. All she could see was candy wrappers, fluff and a grit-caked lollipop, but no Theo.

"What's the matter?" came Ma's voice from the front of the busmarine.

Bea stood up slowly and turned to face her. She did not want to meet her mother's eye. She opened her mouth, but it was a struggle to get the words out.

"It's Theo," she said. "He's gone."

# Listening

Through the moonlit forest crept a blank-faced boy named Ike Ledbetter. He was twelve years old, or maybe fourteen, or nine. He had never been able to grasp numbers, which buzzed around his head and refused to settle long enough to make sense. At the first sign of the moon changing he had been sent to Cambio Falls to spy on the new arrivals. He slipped barefoot through the woods. The soles of his feet were leathery and hard. When he walked on stone floors it sounded as if he were wearing shoes, but among the trees he was the quietest of a stealthy clan.

Well before he reached the waterfall he knew that something was amiss. The birds were passing alarms to one another when they should have been settling down for the night, and he could hear tiny shouts carried on the breeze. "Ee-oh," he heard, repeated in several voices, some high and some low. As he got closer the word turned into *Theo*. He wondered who Theo could be, and why he was being summoned so urgently. How many things could there be that wouldn't wait until tomorrow? None of the voices he could hear was familiar to him, and his curiosity drew him closer to the sound.

When he reached the edge of the trees he stopped behind a trunk to size up the situation. Bontoc was back, as expected, and he had a new busload of strangers with him. There was always a certain amount of shouting and upset when strangers arrived, and Bontoc was well used to it, but Ike saw that it was different this time. The captain would usually be leading the way along the path to Bell Hoot by now, but instead he was sitting on a mossy rock by the falls, scratching his head in a puzzled fashion. A thin lady was shouting at him, her arms waving about like spider's legs and her face just inches from his. She had drawings on her skin.

"That's not good enough!" she was yelling. "You brought us here. You *must* know where he could be. He can't have just *vanished*!"

There was an enormous splash from the pool. Someone had jumped in, but Ike did not see who it was. It sounded like a water buffalo. A skinny girl followed the first splash, leaping into the water as though there were no oilsnakes or slimfish to worry about. There were more people still on the Blue Moon Mobile, pulling up the seat cushions and tossing suitcases out onto the grassy bank, and still shouting for Theo. Evidently Theo was lost. But how could you lose someone on the Blue Moon Mobile?

An old lady appeared suddenly beside Ike, giving him the fright of his life. It's not easy to sneak up on someone who's an expert at sneaking up on people, and since Ike was just such an expert he was not used to being caught in this way. The old lady had big round eyes like a nightbird's, and she grabbed his wrist with a strong grip. Her expression was determined.

"Where do children go," she said in an urgent whisper, "who are lost in the crossing?"

Ike Ledbetter shook his head. "I never heard of it happening before, ma'am," he said. "It's just the cats and frogs and parakeets that disappear, usually."

The old lady's grip loosened. She looked beaten for a moment; then she pulled herself together. "What's your name?" she asked, fixing him with a keen eye.

Ike was taken aback. He was supposed to be finding out about the new people, not the other way around. Still, he could not think of a tricky answer in time, and the truth came out instead. Some of it, anyway. "Ike, ma'am," he said. "Just Ike."

"Well, Just Ike," said the old lady, "if you see a small boy on your travels, bring him to Captain Bontoc. Don't let him out of your sight. You know Captain Bontoc, I presume?"

Ike nodded. He felt pretty sure he'd be in deep trouble if he did what the lady asked, but it didn't seem a good thing to mention that now. "Okay," he said, and since the conversation seemed to be at an end, he turned and disappeared swiftly among the trees.

On board the Blue Moon Mobile, Bea Flint was standing on her tiptoes on the bench where Theo had last been seen. She could just see over the metal lip of the overhead luggage rack. There was no Theo there, either, just a thick layer of dust that made her sneeze so hard she almost fell backward off the seat. Outside the busmarine Ma was still shouting at the bewildered Captain Bontoc.

"Then bring us back through!" she yelled. "He must have gotten off the bus before . . . before we went into that *thing*!"

"We can't go back through," said Bontoc. He gestured

at the pale blue moon as though that explained every-thing. "It's too late."

"Now then," came Granny Delphine's stern voice, "it seems that Theo is not on the bus and not in the water. Where else could he be?"

Bontoc would not meet Granny Delphine's eye. "Disappeared," he said. He wiped his brow with his sleeve. "Must have had a pet hidden. Him or one of the other kids, but up till now it's always been the animal that goes pop. Never the child." He looked up sud-denly. "He wasn't *asleep*, was he?"

"Asleep?" said Ma. "What if he was? What do you mean, 'disappeared'? Disappeared where?"

"We don't know," he said. "Somewhere between here and the Other Side. All that's left usually is a meow or a cheep, trapped in the Squeak Jar. Nobody knows how it happens, but nine souls is the limit. Always has been."

"We didn't have any pets with us," said Ma. "We left the neighbors in charge of Theo's meerkat."

Bea stepped down slowly from the bench. A cold tide of dread and guilt was rising in her chest. She reached out for Theo's backpack and quietly opened the zipper a couple of inches. A nose poked out immediately like a twitching brown button. Bea glanced at Gabby, who was crawling mechanically toward the front of the bus, her head swiveling as she looked under each seat in turn. Bea pushed the meerkat's nose gently back inside and closed the zipper. She had known that Theo intended to smuggle Nails in his backpack. No, she admitted to herself, it was more than that. She had helped him at the last minute to line the backpack with a plastic bag and stock it with food for the trip. Now Theo was gone, and Nails remained. Could Bontoc be right about the reason for Theo's disappearance? Could she really be to blame?

She pushed the idea to the back of her mind with a great effort and looked out of the window. Clockwork Gabby was ratcheting across the grass now, holding the thick glass jar out toward the captain. Bea slung the backpack over her shoulder and followed her outside. Before Gabby could hand over the jar, Ma grabbed it from her with a wild look in her eyes, and began to unscrew the lid.

Bontoc leaped to his feet. "Don't open it!" he yelped. He rummaged in his pocket and produced a small wooden horn with a flat end, like the one a midwife uses to listen to a baby's heartbeat. It had BLUE MOON

ONCE-IN-A-LIFETIME ADVENTURE HOLIDAYS stamped in gold lettering down one side, and it looked something like this:

He took the Squeak Jar from Ma's shaking hand, and placed the mouth of the horn on the lid and the flat end to his ear. Bea, Gabby, Ma and Granny Delphine watched him closely. In the pool behind them Bald Mountain surfaced for a moment, spat out a stream of water, spluttered, "THEO!" for good measure, and submerged again.

"Well?" whispered Ma.

Captain Bontoc shook his head. "Nothing," he said.

Ma's knees buckled suddenly and she sat down heavily in the grass.

"Let me try," said Bea. She put the end of the horn to her ear and held her breath.

Now, the pool at the foot of Cambio Falls is not the quietest of places at the best of times, and on this particular night it was noisier than usual. Thirty tons of water per minute thundering into a pool make a hissing roar that you could hide a lot of smaller sounds in. Add to that the rustling of a million leaves, the creaking of branches, the chirping of blats, the who-hooting of howls, and a 250-pound man surfacing from the churning water and blowing like a whale every sixty seconds, and it would take an extraordinarily good listener to find in that din the voice of a lost boy with two missing teeth.

As luck would have it, Bea had always been an extraordinarily good listener. What was more, she knew from experience that if Theo needed to be heard he would find a way. She closed her eyes and put her finger in her free ear. One by one she drew aside the sounds she did not want, like a series of curtains, until right in the middle of the noise she heard a voice. It was thin and faint but unmistakably Theo's.

"What am I going to do *now*?" said the voice.

"Theo!" whispered Bea, as loudly as she dared. She felt her voice should match the volume of Theo's in order to reach him, although that didn't seem entirely logical. There was no answer from Theo, but she could still hear him sniffling somewhere in the distance.

"Can you hear him?" asked Captain Bontoc.

Bea nodded, not wanting to take her ear from the horn.

"Quick," said Bontoc in a loud whisper, "ask him to describe where he is."

"Where are you, Theo?" asked Bea. Despite the seriousness of the situation she felt slightly foolish speaking to a jar.

She strained to hear Theo's voice again. In the background she could hear Bontoc whispering eagerly to Gabby, "If we can find the boy we might find my parrot, Trigger. Lost him on my first crossing thirty years ago."

"Right here, of course," said Theo's voice, even fainter than before. "Where are we?"

Bea took her ear from the horn. It was a good question. "Where exactly are we?" she asked Captain Bontoc.

Ma took the jar from Bea before Bontoc could answer. She put her ear slowly to the horn, as though expecting to hear nothing, and wanting to put off the moment of disappointment. She listened for a long time, then looked up at Bea and shook her head. "It's the shock," she said, and she got unsteadily to her feet. Her voice was trembling. "It's playing tricks with your imagination."

"I *heard* him!" said Bea. "I'm sure of it." She was not so sure of it, really. It did seem unlikely that her missing brother's voice would be speaking from a glass jar with a screw-top lid.

Captain Bontoc tugged the creases from his blazer and attempted an air of authority. "Best thing is to get ourselves to Bell Hoot at once and consult the chart. Wherever he is, he has to show up on the chart. Follow me, if you please. Look lively!" He scooped up a number of cases, balancing some on his head and shoulders. He was about to start up the path when he was arrested by a bellow from the edge of the pool.

"Where do you think you're going?" spluttered Bald Mountain. He was clinging to a rock, half in and half out of the water, trying to regain his breath. Pond water ran from his nostrils and soaked into his bushy beard.

"You won't find the boy in the water, sir," replied Captain Bontoc. "The Blue Moon Mobile is completely sealed when she's under. Couldn't get an amoeba in or out of her. Tight as a drum, she is."

Ma stared around her quickly, as though a last look might reveal Theo standing right there by the bus; then she turned and marched rapidly after the captain, the Squeak Jar clutched tightly under her arm, despite its apparent emptiness. The others followed, stumbling up the path with whatever they could carry, Pa and Phoebe leaving trails of silvery water behind them in the moonlight. The path crested a rise, and they could see pointed roofs among the trees ahead of them.

Ma had drawn ahead of Captain Bontoc, who nonetheless kept up a surprising pace under the weight of an entire family's luggage.

Pa muttered testily at the rear. "Don't see why we couldn't bring the bus," he said.

"Too noisy," called Captain Bontoc over his shoulder. "It might attract . . . might wake people up, shipmate."

They strode into the moonlit village, the captain and the tattooed lady setting the pace. Behind them came Bea Flint, her silver-haired granny, her enormous father, their clockwork lodger and the neighbors' girl, Phoebe Lu, who had yet to meet anything she feared.

"Beanos," said Gabby as she clicked along. It was the first word she had spoken for many years, and her disused voice was no more than a whisper. Nobody heard but Bea, and she was so sure she must be mistaken that she didn't stop to wonder what it could mean.

Most of the wooden houses in the village were built about ten feet from the ground, supported by sturdy trees, as though their occupants feared that a river might change course and rush through the village at any moment. Chickens scratched around underneath the houses, and here and there pigs slumbered in the shadows. In the center of the village stood a large square building of pale gray stone, and it was to this building that Captain Bontoc was striding like an overladen ant. There were tall windows at intervals around the building. Above the door the words BELL HOOT LIBRARY were chiseled into the stone lintel.

The captain climbed the few steps to the door and deposited the luggage in an untidy pile. He fumbled in his pocket for a key, but Ma could not stand the wait. She planted her finger on the doorbell and held it there, while the shrill bell echoed inside the building. Bea glimpsed an expression on her face that she was more used to seeing on Granny Delphine's. Granny

Delphine was frowning and muttering to herself, and Pa kicked angrily at the top step as though it were the stone's fault that his little boy had vanished.

*What will happen to us all*, Bea found herself wondering, *if we never see Theo again?*

# Squeeze

**C**aptain Bontoc opened the door into the library and flicked on the lights. "Follow me," he said. He passed between rows of silent books and hurried up a staircase that climbed the wall at the rear, with Ma following at his heels and the others close behind. At the top of the stairs the captain opened the door to a small office. The lights were on inside, and to Bea's surprise she could hear the clacking of an old typewriter.

"Someone's working late," muttered Pa.

They shuffled in through the narrow door, all except for Phoebe, who could not resist sliding back down the banister, oblivious to the sheer drop beside it.

The office was a small room in the attic of the building. It had a sloping ceiling with wooden beams. Two desks stood side by side in the middle of the room, and at the far wall was a long bench. A number of people sat there in the gloom. Most of them seemed to be asleep.

On one of the desks sat an iron typewriter that must have been at least fifty years old. A woman of around the same age was tapping away at it with fingers like dancing sausages. "Won't be a second!" she called out, without looking up. "I'm just typing up your cards."

Captain Bontoc strode to the larger desk and unrolled a chart that lay on the desktop. He leaned forward, frowning, and began to trace the lines with a bitten fingernail. Bea looked at the chart with interest. As far as she could see it was an exact copy of the one that the brush-haired man had been filling out at the car wash. She was sure she even recognized some of the strange little annotations the man had made in between the planets. It seemed a long time ago.

"Will the chart show us where Theo is?" she asked the captain.

"The little tyke's gotten himself lost already, has he?" said the lady at the typewriter. She looked up and smiled. She had a double chin and gaps between her teeth. She seemed to know who Theo was.

"Not exactly, Miss 'opkins," said Captain Bontoc. "Boy disappeared on the crossing."

Miss Hopkins stopped typing and her smile grew puzzled. "*On* the crossing?" she repeated. "That's impossible!"

"Of course it's impossible," snapped Ma. She turned to Captain Bontoc. "You said yourself the bus was sealed. He must have gotten off before we started. He's still at the car wash, and I demand you take us back at once." She folded her arms and glared. "He's barely *seven*."

Captain Bontoc looked up from the chart. "You're in luck," he said with a nervous smile. "There'll be another crossing in three weeks."

"Three *weeks*?" said Ma sharply.

The lady at the typewriter flinched, and those on the bench who were still asleep woke up with a start.

"Have you found him on the chart?" asked Bea.

Captain Bontoc scratched his head. "Afraid not, missy. I only know how to plot a crossing, really. Mr. Waxy's the one who interprets the chart. He'll find the boy for sure. Everyone has to be somewhere."

"But we can't wait three weeks!" said Ma. "What will happen to Theo in the meantime?"

"Nothing, ma'am. Long as young . . . Bea can hear him we know he's safe." He gestured at a shelf behind him, where another large jar perched among the dusty books. "My parrot Trigger's still going strong after thirty years. I talk to him often. Can't tell me where he is, that's the problem."

Bea could feel Nails the meerkat shifting in the backpack that she carried over her shoulder, and the guilty feeling in her chest shifted with him. She knew she should tell the captain that the meerkat had survived the crossing, but she could not pluck up the courage. She was afraid of what Granny Delphine would say to her, and more than that she dreaded facing her mother with the news that Bea herself might somehow be responsible for Theo's disappearance.

"Why don't you just phone him?" said Ma. "Mr. Waxy, or whatever he calls himself."

"Phone him?" said Bontoc. "*Phone* him?" He looked at Granny Delphine as though for help, but the old lady's lips were thin and she appeared to be staring at the rafters. "There . . . er . . . isn't a phone line to the Other Side," said Bontoc. He clapped his hands together briskly. "Now, if you'll just wait for a moment we'll sort you out with—"

He got no further with what he was saying. Without anyone noticing, Pa's face had been turning slowly redder, like an iron in the fire. Now it had reached a rich plum color. He started toward the captain. Bea stepped hurriedly to one side. Pa had been famous for his bear hugs back in the days when he rode with the Flying Rascals Motorcycle Club. Legend had it that when Bald Mountain put the squeeze on somebody they came around very rapidly to his point of view. Indeed, there were many people who had found themselves a good deal thinner after a disagreement with Bald Mountain than they had been before.

He stepped around behind Captain Bontoc with surprising nimbleness. He picked the captain clean off the floor in his massive tattooed arms, and he began to squeeze. Bea winced. Ma looked triumphant, as though she expected the solutions to all their problems to be squeezed out of the captain like toothpaste. Bea stole a look at Granny Delphine and so she missed what happened when Bald Mountain achieved maximum squeeze. From the corner of her eye she caught a glimpse of the captain giving a mighty wriggle. A croaking sound escaped him. His shiny skin and whiskered face gave a fleeting impression of a plump seal escaping from a trawler net, and a moment later he was free.

There was chaos in the room. The typewriter woman

let out a delayed shriek. Captain Bontoc, now standing several feet away from Pa, shook himself back into
shape. Pa was hugging himself, a surprised look replacing the anger on his face, and there was a nervous
rumble from the people on the bench.

It was at this point that Granny Delphine took com-
mand. "*Enough!*" she said in a shrill voice.

Everything stopped.

"There's nothing more we can do tonight." She
swept the room with her owl eyes, and even the strangers fell silent. "It seems that Theo is in no immedi-
ate danger. In the morning we will organize a proper
search, and in the meantime Captain Bontoc will show
us where we are to stay."

"Ah, yes," said the captain. He turned to the typewriter lady. "If you please, Miss 'opkins?"

Miss Hopkins opened a drawer in her desk. She
took out a small wooden box, placed it carefully on the
corner of the desk, and opened it. The people on the
bench shifted nervously. One of them, a stooped man
in a shapeless felt hat, stood up hastily and addressed the
typewriter woman. "Beg your pardon, Miss Hopkins.
I'd like to be excused from the line. Just remembered
I've got to get the plumegranates in this week."

"Aye," said a woman sitting at the end. "And I've got to get my ears adjusted on Tuesday. I'll volunteer another time."

"Nonsense!" said Miss Hopkins brightly. She tapped the box with a pudgy finger. A large striped grasshopper appeared, first his long curling antennae, then a triangular green head with eyes like coffee beans. He climbed out of the box in a leisurely fashion and surveyed the row of people on the bench. The man in the hat sat down quickly. The people shrank slowly into their collars, and Bea had the distinct impression that they were all trying to avoid catching the grasshopper's attention. The insect made up his mind. He jumped suddenly and flew across the room with a clatter of wings, landing squarely on the felt hat of the man with the plumegranates. The man muttered something under his breath. The rest of the people looked relieved.

"Mr. Miller," said Miss Hopkins. "You're the lucky host!"

Mr. Miller stood up. A reluctant smile broke across his wrinkled face, and he walked forward and stuck out a large bony hand. "Welcome to Bell Hoot," he said. The grasshopper was still perched on his hat.

Ma looked at him blankly, her eyes rimmed with

tears. Bea shook hands with the man instead.

"You'll be staying with the Millers until we get you settled," said Captain Bontoc.

Ma and Pa said nothing. It seemed the fight had gone out of them. Ma looked tired and pale, and there was a thin streamer of pond weed glued to Pa's cheek.

They filed out through the narrow door and down the wooden staircase, following Mr. Miller out into the warm, chirping night. Bea thought about the peculiar animals she had glimpsed on the brochure through Granny Delphine's spectacles, teeming in the undergrowth. A thrill of excitement made her forget for a moment about Theo. She ran a few steps to catch up with their host.

"Are there any big animals here?" she asked in a loud whisper.

"Some," said Mr. Miller. He held up a lantern that cast a pool of light around them. His head turned from side to side, peering into the darkness between the trees. He seemed distracted.

"Where are we going?" asked Bea. "Is it a sort of guesthouse?"

Mr. Miller shook his head. "It's our home."

"Do you normally have lodgers?"

"Nope. It's our turn, is all. You'll get your own place by and by."

"We're only here for three weeks."

Mr. Miller gave Bea a strange look. He seemed about to say something, then thought better of it.

"That's enough questions for now," said Granny Delphine at her shoulder.

Bea heard her mother's voice from the darkness behind. "I have a few questions of my own," she muttered, "and there had better be some answers."

# Lifetime

The Millers' house was perched among the spreading branches of a massive plane tree. It looked like a collection of boxes wedged into the tree wherever they would fit, topped with slanted roofs that jutted out in all directions. A broad verandah stretched along the front of the house, overlooking the small clearing that separated it from the path. The verandah was about fifteen feet from the ground and was bathed in the warm light of a couple of lamps dangling from the overhanging roof. Bea could see no obvious way of reaching it.

Mr. Miller stepped through a gap in the encircling bushes and looked up at the house. "Ladder," he said quietly. Nothing happened. He put his lantern down carefully at his feet and placed his hands on his hips. "Ladder," he said again. The end of a ladder inched out from the verandah and stopped. "Come on!" said Mr. Miller impatiently, and Bea wondered if whoever was pushing it minded being spoken to so abruptly. The ladder inched out farther, then tipped and unfolded suddenly in a series of hinged sections. The last section thumped to the ground at Mr. Miller's feet. "Follow me," he said over his shoulder, and began to climb.

He led them from the verandah into an odd-shaped living room with a large table in the middle. The table was spread with a white cloth, on which a teapot and a stack of plates stood.

Mrs. Miller bustled in from the kitchen at that moment with a dish in each hand and another perched precariously on her head. She had a long neck and fine narrow features like bone china. She smiled when she saw Bea and Phoebe. "Well, well, how nice to have company. I'm Mrs. Miller, but you can call me Gladys. You must be worn out. Here's your mother now. Hello, dear, I'm Gladys; welcome to our house. I'm sorry it's a bit of a pigsty; we're never sure whose turn it will be. This must be your husband. It's a pleasure to meet you. What a magnificent beard, if you don't mind my saying so . . ." Mrs. Miller produced a constant stream of words without seeming to take a breath, all the while dealing out dishes and cutlery like an expert cardplayer, and scurrying in and out of the kitchen with plates of cooked meats and fruit and biscuits and steaming vegetables. She straightened pictures and cushions and replaced books on their shelves as she swept past them. When her hands were already full things seemed to straighten themselves at a mere nod from Mrs. Miller.

"Sit, everyone, please," she said as she swept back in, ducking slightly to avoid a thick branch that passed through one corner of the room. The Flint family seated themselves around the table. Mr. Miller came in from the verandah dusting his hands.

A puzzled look came over Mrs. Miller's porcelain face. "Let me see," she said, "one, two, three, four, five, six, Captain Bontoc, how are you? Mr. Miller and myself, of course, that's nine. Now, who are we missing?"

"Boygone," said Clockwork Gabby, and this time everyone heard her. There was a stunned silence.

"She spoke," said Pa.

"Is that unusual?" asked Mrs. Miller politely.

"Hasn't said a word in years," said Pa, running his hand over his scalp with a puzzled expression.

Mr. Miller put his hand on his wife's arm and said something quietly in her ear. Mrs. Miller's eyes opened wide. "On the crossing?" she said. She looked at Ma sympathetically, and for a second even she was lost for words. "I'm sure he'll be found," she said when she had recovered her tongue. "I don't know much about it, but he must be on the chart, mustn't he, Captain? Have a little bite to eat; it will keep your strength up. Some potatoes, dear? Who'd like a slice of pie?"

"How about you, Gabby?" said Pa with a wink. Gabby said nothing.

Mrs. Miller served everyone around the table at a spectacular pace, and though she had only two hands and a couple of large serving spoons, Bea was sure that most of the food distributed itself under Mrs. Miller's instruction. "More soup?" she said, and the soup level in Pa's bowl rose while the level in the tureen fell a little. Dollops of steaming cabbage leaped onto the plates as soon as they were offered, and when Phoebe wrinkled up her nose at the sight of it, her dollop jumped back hastily into the dish. Bea lifted the cloth and looked under the table to see if there were magnets or pulleys or something. She saw only knees. She looked at the empty chair across the table from her, and suddenly she was too tired to wonder about it anymore.

"Had enough?" said Mrs. Miller, who missed nothing. "I'll show you where you'll be sleeping. The beds have just been made up fresh. Up the stairs with you, this way, watch your head."

Bea was almost too tired to undress. She expected to fall asleep the moment her head hit the pillow, but sleep didn't come so easily. The bed was softer than she was accustomed to, and the mattress sagged under her in an alarming way. Strange squeaks and hoots came from the forest outside her window, punctuated by the slow, rhythmic *creeeak . . . squik . . . creeeak . . . squik* of the house as it swayed gently in the treetop. She held Theo's backpack close to her under the blanket. She had opened the zipper slightly to give the meerkat air, but she was afraid to let him out.

The events of the night swirled around and around in her head. The busmarine, the car wash, the awful sucking pop of her little brother's disappearance, the unwelcoming welcome committee in the office above the library, Mrs. Miller and her obedient supper. She almost felt angry at Theo for spoiling what should have been an extraordinary start to a holiday, but as soon as the thought entered her head a lump appeared in her throat and she had to squeeze her eyes shut. She hugged the backpack closer, and drifted into a restless sleep.

She found herself at home in her familiar bedroom, sitting on the edge of the bed. The room was smaller somehow. The floor felt soft and spongy beneath her feet.

"What am I going to do now?" said Theo's voice. It sounded just as she had heard it from the Squeak Jar, but without all the background noise.

"Theo?" she said. "Where are you?"

"Here."

"Are you hiding under the bed?" said Bea. She was afraid to look between her ankles. "It's not funny. Everyone's looking for you."

"What would I be doing under the bed?" said Theo. She could tell he wasn't lying, and she got the uncomfortable feeling that he might be somewhere outside the window, even though they lived on the third floor. Or was it the thirtieth? She couldn't quite remember.

"Are we going back to the busmarine soon?" said Theo's voice. "I left Nails there."

"Nails is with me," said Bea. She had a flash of inspiration. "If you can tell me where you are I'll bring him to you."

There was a pause. "Is this a game? Do you have him hidden?"

"Yes," said Bea. "Nobody else knows. Can you tell me where you are?"

"Ummmm," said Theo, "on holiday?"

Bea felt frustration rising in her. She didn't seem to be getting anywhere. "What does the place look like? It's not like a . . . like a big glass jar or anything?"

There was a splutter of laughter from Theo, followed by an angry shout of *"Never?"* The shout came not from Theo but from Ma, and it dispersed Bea's dream like a puff of smoke. She could feel the bedsprings bouncing beneath her, so suddenly had she jerked awake. There were voices from the verandah below her window. She could hear Ma's voice, and Granny Delphine's, and another voice that must have been Captain Bontoc's. She could not make out what they were saying. *I bet it's not as important as what I was asking Theo*, she thought.

"Phoebe?" she said. "Are you asleep?"

"I would be if you weren't talking to me."

"I dreamed about Theo."

"What did you dream?" said Phoebe.

"Besides the obvious, you mean?"

"Yes."

"I dreamed I was in my room back home. I could hear Theo but much clearer than . . . than from the jar."

"What did he say?"

"I was trying to find out where he is, but I woke up before he could tell me."

"Why did you do that?"

"I didn't wake up *deliberately*! I heard Ma shout. I think she's having a fight with Granny Delphine."

She heard Phoebe's bare feet land on the floorboards.

"Where are you going?" she said.

"I'm going to see what they're talking about."

Bea got out of her bed too without a word. She quietly closed the zipper on Theo's backpack and put it over her shoulder. She could see Phoebe's silhouette as she slipped out through the door. She crept down the stairs after her. It was an unfamiliar staircase, so she did not know which ones might creak. Phoebe was skipping every second step, but the ones she did choose let out loud creaks anyway. Bea carefully stepped on the ones her friend had avoided, which creaked just as loudly. Together they sounded like a pair of giant crickets walking a polished corridor in new shoes.

The door to the verandah stood open. Ma, Granny Delphine, Captain Bontoc and Pa sat on cane chairs in a pool of lamplight. Pa had nodded off. There was no sign of Clockwork Gabby or the Millers. "I *couldn't* have told you," Granny Delphine was saying. "You wouldn't have come."

"You're darn right I wouldn't!" said Ma angrily. "And we're going right back, just as soon as we find Theo. I've done nothing wrong."

"That won't make any difference to the Gummint, love. You know that."

Bea followed Phoebe, tiptoeing across the darkened dining room toward the table where Mrs. Miller had served them supper. The Squeak Jar stood in the center of the table, reflecting the yellow glow of the lamplight outside. Captain Bontoc's listening horn lay beside it. They sat down quietly to eavesdrop.

"They can't arrest *all* of us. We've never had anything to do with Mumbo Jumbo," Ma was saying.

"They can and they will. Whole families disappear every day. Most are never seen again. The Gummint sees Mumbo Jumbo as a danger to society. They're afraid of it."

"Mrs. Walker's right," said Captain Bontoc. "It's said they carry out experiments on their prisoners, trying to find out ways to eradicate Mumbo Jumbo altogether. Once they suspect someone of being a Pearlseed they'll arrest the entire family. They sent men to pick you up last night. You got out just in time."

Ma shook her head slowly. "I'll find my boy, and we'll all go home on the next crossing."

Captain Bontoc sighed. "If I know the Gummint men there'll be nothing left of your home. They've never been able to discover where Pearlseeds escape to, and they'll tear the place apart looking for clues. It'll look like a plague of locusts held their annual jamboree there, believe me."

"I'm not going to spend the rest of my life in hiding," said Ma. She wore a stubborn look. "You'll just have to bring us back."

"Impossible, I'm afraid, ma'am," said the captain. He took a gulp of rum and set his glass down on the low table in front of him. "'Sky black, moon blue, nine souls go through.'"

"What's that supposed to mean?" asked Ma.

"What it says," said Captain Bontoc. "When the moon turns blue on the Other Side the crossing is open. Nine souls can go through, no more, no less."

"The moon is still blue," said Ma.

Captain Bontoc looked up at the sky. "Course it is, ma'am," he said patiently. "It's always blue on this side, except when it turns blue on the Other Side, of course.

Then it turns yellow here, if you follow me."

"And we were only seven," said Ma.

"Right again, ma'am. Seven passengers, myself, and Captain Fuller making the reverse crossing. Seven arriving and two driving makes nine."

"We'll still be seven on the way back. Six, if my mother decides to stay here."

Captain Bontoc pursed his lips. "There'll be more coming through," he said. "Crossing's only open once in a blue moon, and not for long at that. We bring a family through every time, and it's still not enough. There are no return trips."

"You can't *do* that to us!" said Ma. "We came here on a holiday!"

Captain Bontoc smiled cheerfully. "Window dressing, ma'am. Blue Moon Once-in-a-Lifetime Adventure Holidays is a cover story. Helps to keep our operation under wraps, as well as persuading the . . . er . . . reluctant traveler. It did say 'the holiday of a lifetime' in the brochure."

Granny Delphine reached out and put her hand on Ma's knee. "I'm sorry," she said.

In the darkened living room Bea looked at Phoebe in astonishment. She could see Phoebe's eyebrows raised too. Granny Delphine was Always Right, and an apology from her was even rarer than a blue moon.

"It was the only way," said Granny Delphine. "We were all in danger, but you would never have let me persuade you."

"And what about Theo? What about Phoebe?"

"Theo would have been taken by the Gummint anyway, along with the rest of us. He's safer where he is. If Bea can hear him, she can help us find him. She just needs some training. As for Phoebe . . ." She blinked behind her big round spectacles. "That wasn't an easy decision, but I take full responsibility."

Ma sat up straight in her chair. "You've made us into kidnappers, that's what you've done. And as for your so-called training, we've been through this a hundred times. You're not filling my daughter's head with Mumbo Jumbo. It's brought us nothing but trouble so far."

"It may be the only way," said Granny Delphine, "to bring Theo back."

# Freezalizer

**B**ea Flint sneaked a biscuit from a plate that sat in the center of the table. She had not had a moment to look for worms to give to Nails, and she knew he must be hungry. Worms were among the meerkat's favorite dishes, but the mere idea of feeding them to him made Bea's skin crawl. Biscuits were not nearly so good for him, but at least she did not have to imagine them silently screaming as his sharp little teeth crunched them up.

She opened the zipper on the backpack just enough to fit the biscuit through. Unfortunately a gap that will just fit a large biscuit will also just fit a small meerkat. Nails was tired of being cooped up in the dark, and when he heard the zipper opening he grabbed his chance. He was out of the bag and running across the moon-striped floor before you could say "escaped meerkat."

"Ndah!" said Bea. It was one of those meaning-less words that come out when you are taken so much by surprise that your tongue gets ahead of your brain. Out on the lamplit verandah Granny Delphine looked around for a moment and frowned into the darkened living room before returning to the conversation.

Phoebe stared after the fugitive meerkat in astonish-ment. "That's Nails!" she whispered loudly.

"I *know* that!" said Bea. She grabbed another biscuit from the plate and crept across the floor, following the direction that Nails had taken. Through the open back door she could see him running along the edge of the back porch, looking for a route to the ground. "Nails!" whispered Bea, making kissing noises with her lips. "Come here, Nails. I've got bikkies. Nice bikkies."

The meerkat stood up and looked back at her. His head ducked up and down as he examined the biscuit. He had been too busy escaping to eat the one that she had posted into the stuffy backpack, but his hunger made this one look particularly biscuity, and escape didn't seem so urgent now that he was in the open air. He turned and took a few steps back toward her, but at that moment Phoebe appeared on the porch. Nails knew an ambush when he saw one. He ran back along the porch and took a flying leap at a slender branch that stretched out from a neighboring tree and ended several feet away. He scrabbled for purchase among the dancing leaves; then he was off along the branch and down the trunk in the blink of an eye. Biscuits were all very well, the meerkat was thinking, but his usual boy gave him worms and beetles. He had no idea where Theo was, but he had a good sense of direction and his priorities were clear. Worms and beetles would be back on the menu if he had any say in the matter.

Bea sat back on her heels on the back porch, fifteen feet above the ground. "I almost had him," she hissed.

"But how did he get here?" asked Phoebe. She held the Squeak Jar under one arm, and the end of the listening horn poked out of her pocket.

"How do you think?" said Bea. She was too annoyed to worry about trying to keep her secret. "He came in Theo's backpack."

"I thought we weren't supposed to bring pets," said Phoebe.

"We couldn't very well leave him with . . ." Bea looked at Phoebe and stopped herself. " . . . on his own," she finished. She turned quickly and looked down into the moonlit clearing. Nails was looking back over his shoulder from a little way along the path. He knew if he stopped and waited Bea would come after him. He was not about to be caught just yet, but he didn't want to get lost either.

"We have to go after him," said Bea. They lowered the ladder—another jointed one like the one that Mr. Miller had called down from the front verandah—being careful not to make any noise. Bea put the jar and the horn into Theo's backpack.

"We'd better put the ladder back up," Bea whispered when they reached the ground.

Phoebe shook her head. "They might hear us."

"They're too busy arguing."

"Except your pa. He's too busy snoring."

Bea put her hand over her mouth to stop herself from laughing, which made snot come out of her nose instead.

"Mr. Miller seemed pretty worried about pulling it up after us when we arrived," she insisted when she had recovered herself.

Phoebe shrugged. "Okay." She ran silently back up the ladder and began to haul it up after her.

"Yes, but how will you—," began Bea, but Phoebe had already stowed the ladder and launched herself into the air. She landed on the soft earth with a thump—a small one—and sprang back up like a gymnast ending her routine.

"Let's go!" she said. They followed Nails along the path that led back toward Cambio Falls. The meerkat kept his distance, but he stopped every now and then and looked back to make sure they were following him. The moon hung near the horizon, as fat and blue as a tropical fish, and their shadows stretched out behind them like slender marionettes.

They passed between the dark silhouettes of houses perched like angular bird nests in the trees on either side of the path. Lamps burned outside some of them, but there was no sign that anyone else was awake.

"What do you think they're afraid of?" said Phoebe.

"Who says they're afraid?" said Bea.

"Look at all those thornbushes."

Bea peered into the shadows beneath the tree houses. "What about them?"

"They're always right below the windows." Phoebe saw most things in terms of the opportunities they presented for jumping, climbing or dangerous feats of acrobatics. She had noticed right away that it would be difficult to do any of those things around these houses, unless you wanted to end up looking like you had sat on a porcupine.

"Maybe they get a lot of burglars," said Bea.

The path was sloping gently downward now. The number of houses dwindled to nothing, and the trees grew closer together. The meerkat stayed ten leaps ahead, his tail standing up like an antenna. The night did not get quieter as they left the town behind. On the contrary, the farther they got from Bell Hoot the more it sounded like a miniature metropolis was hidden among the trees. On all sides there was a symphony of squeaks and clicks, coughs and whistles, hooting and hissing and the occasional distant howl. Dry leaves rustled with the passing of little claws and the swishing of tails, and nightbirds floated silently through the darkness, flapping only when they had to.

Phoebe stopped and grabbed Bea's arm so suddenly that she almost jumped out of her skin. She pointed into the shadows beneath the trees, and Bea caught a glimpse of a pair of large round eyes staring out at them. The eyes blinked, and for a moment she thought she saw the shape of a boy slipping away into the darkness.

"Someone's spying on us," said Phoebe.

"Maybe it was just a monkey," said Bea doubtfully.

Phoebe laughed. "Monkeys don't wear hats!" she said. She plunged into the bushes where the boy had been a moment before. "Let's follow him," she called.

"We can't," said Bea. "We'll lose Nails." She looked along the path and saw the meerkat lolloping along toward the falls. Phoebe had already vanished among the trees. "Phoebe!" she called urgently. "We have to go. And we don't know who's in there."

"You go ahead," came Phoebe's voice. "I'll catch up." The nocturnal racket had intensified around her as birds scolded, and the ground shook with what sounded like startled rabbits thumping their alarms.

Bea was torn between the desire to follow Phoebe into the thick of the teeming forest and the urgency of following Nails. There was no real choice, of course. All they had left of Theo was his disembodied voice and the rapidly receding meerkat, and if she lost sight of Nails she might never see him again. "Don't go far," she called after Phoebe. She rejoined the path. She felt nervous now on her own. The path seemed less welcoming, and the leaves muttered in the night breeze.

Nails was far ahead now, and she had to hurry to catch up with him. She kept her ears open for any sign of Phoebe. After a while she noticed a soft hum behind all the noise. She could not tell what it was, but it brought to her mind's eye a picture of sunlight, put to rest somewhere for the night but never quite sleeping. She took some comfort from it, but no matter how she strained she could not hear it more clearly. As she approached the falls the sound was drowned out by the growing roar of the water.

Where the path emerged from the trees Nails paused and stood up straight like a miniature security guard. His whiskers twitched and his pointed nose turned from side to side as he surveyed the area. The Blue Moon Mobile stood silently by the water's edge as though it hadn't moved in years. The meerkat ran toward it. When he reached the busmarine he stood and placed his front paws against the curved metal hull.

"Theo's not there," said Bea quietly.

The meerkat looked back at her, and Bea could have sworn he jerked his head as though beckoning to her. She rubbed her eyes and crept closer to where Nails stood. She was afraid that he would run away if she got too near, but his eyes seemed to be fixed on the Blue Moon Mobile's painted hull. As she neared the busmarine she could see a black line between two of the metal panels below the level of the busmarine's floor. It looked as if a luggage compartment had been left slightly open. She could not be sure in the dim light of the moon, but it seemed the gap was getting gradually wider.

She held her breath and leaned in for a closer look. Two of the screws that held the panel in place were turning by themselves. There was no doubt about it. She could see another couple of screws glinting in the grass beside her, where they had already fallen out. She took in a sharp breath and grabbed Nails just in time. The heavy steel panel fell outward with a dull thud, narrowly missing them both.

A wave of hot stuffy air escaped the dark compartment, and a gasp came with it. Bea's heart missed a beat. "Theo?" she said. There was a scrabbling sound from inside; then a hand quickly emerged. It was a large hand with long articulate fingers. It was certainly not Theo's. Bea's heart plummeted. The hand grasped the top edge of the panel and tried to pull it back into place, but without success. The panel was heavy, and became heavier still when Bea planted her foot on it. The hand withdrew.

"Who's there?" said Bea. "And what have you done with Theo?"

"Theo?" echoed a voice from the darkness.

"Come out where we can see you," said Phoebe

from behind Bea, making her jump.

A head appeared, followed by a long thin body in a pair of dirty overalls. A greasy rag was stuffed half into the breast pocket, and a set of wrenches clinked in a tool belt. The man got to his knees, then straightened up stiffly. His face was round and open. He wore an impressive handlebar mustache that swept up to join a set of thick graying whiskers. His hair was long and slicked back. He looked at the two girls with a befuddled expression. "Am I late?" he said.

"Late for what?" said Phoebe.

"I just came to," said the man. He spoke slowly. "I was fixing the ice-cream machine, but I got my head stuck in the freezalizer. Knocked me out cold." He got slowly to his feet, creaking like a frozen deck chair. "Again," he added ruefully.

"So that's why it wasn't working," said Bea.

The man nodded. "You can only get at it from underneath. It needs a new freezalizer unit, but it has to come from Japan. I keep fixing the old one until it comes. It's a long way from Japan, you know." He looked at Bea and smiled; then his eyes opened wide as he spotted the meerkat struggling in her arms. "Nice doggie!" he said, and his smile grew even wider.

"He's a meerkat," said Bea. She did not know what to make of this man. It was impossible to tell how old he was. He might have been forty or seventy. His face was lined, but there was a childlike innocence in his expression.

"Nice meerkat," said the man. "Nice doggie." He reached out to stroke Nails.

"Careful," said Bea. "He bites strangers." To her surprise the meerkat did nothing of the sort. He stopped wriggling. He pushed his head against the man's hand and allowed himself to be tickled under his chin.

"I'm not a stranger," said the stranger. "I'm Arkadi. Everybody knows Arkadi. I fix things."

"Except when you get your head stuck in the freezalizer," said Bea.

The man nodded again. If he had taken offense he didn't show it. "I only woke up because it thawed out. Lucky I . . ." But he got no further. He caught sight of the moon and the simple smile left his face at once. His jaw dropped open and he stared wildly about him.

"Where are we?" he asked in a loud whisper.

"I think it's called Bell Hoot," said Bea.

"That's the town," said Phoebe.

"Bell Hoot," repeated the stranger, and to look at

him you would think he had just been told he was in a tank of hungry crocodiles. "Uh-oh. I'm in trouble. Big, big trouble."

"I don't think they'll hang you for nearly getting your head turned into ice cream," said Bea.

Arkadi sank down to the ground and sat there cross-legged, his knuckles pressed to his mouth. "I'm not supposed to be here," he said.

"I'm sure it will be okay," said Bea. "We'll bring you back to the Millers' house and . . ." She was about to say she was sure that Captain Bontoc would arrange to have him sent back, but she remembered the conversation on the verandah, and she had a feeling it would not be that simple.

The stranger shook his head violently. "Don't tell anyone," he said. "I'm only supposed to fix the machines."

"It wasn't your fault," said Bea.

"That won't matter," said Arkadi. He stared wide-eyed at the two girls. "Promise you won't tell anyone."

Bea looked at Phoebe. Her arms were scratched and her T-shirt was torn. Phoebe shrugged. "I promise," she said.

Arkadi looked at Bea. "Promise?" he said.

"I promise," she said. She felt sorry for the shivering stranger.

A look of relief came over his face. "Someone must have locked me in," he said.

"Maybe they didn't know you were still in there."

"I'll hide," he said. "That's what I'll do. I can hide in the forest."

"What good will that do?" asked Bea. "You'll have to come out sometime."

Arkadi shook his head. "I'll think of something," he said. He didn't look as though thinking of something was his specialty.

"There's a little hut in the woods," said Phoebe. "I found it just now, when I was looking for the spy. There's some old traps and stuff in it, but it looks like nobody's been there for ages. You could hide there."

"Okay," said the man. He smiled suddenly and put his finger to his lips. He looked at Bea, and back at Nails. "Nice doggie," he said half to himself. He got to his feet, and Phoebe gave him directions—three times over—to the hut she had found. The stranger loped off without another word and vanished from sight.

# Here

"Theo?" said Bea quietly. She sat on the moss-cushioned rock where Captain Bontoc had sat earlier. The listening horn was pressed to the lid of the Squeak Jar, and Bea's ear was pressed to the listening horn. Phoebe crouched in the grass and watched intently, as though she might catch sight of a miniature seven-year-old boy shimmering in the moonlight that filled the jar. The noise at Cambio Falls was as great as ever, but this was where Bea had first heard Theo's disembodied voice, and it seemed the natural place to try to hear it again.

"Anything?" said Phoebe.

"Ssshh!" said Bea. She had located the distant voice, but she had to tune into it before she could make out his words, like a weak radio signal.

"Where did you go?" said Theo's voice.

"I woke up," said Bea. She wasn't sure if the Theo in the Squeak Jar would remember the conversation she had had with the Theo in her dream. She wondered if he would know what she was talking about.

"I don't know what you're talking about," said Theo. "First you were asking if I was in a giant jar, which is a stupid question, I think you'll agree. Then when I looked you were gone. Now you're back."

Bea let this sink in for a moment. "You can *see* me?" she said.

There was a pause. Bea could picture Theo's face, his nose wrinkled with incredulity. "You've gotten really weird since we came on holiday. Of course I can see you. I don't need glasses, you know."

"Can he see us?" said Phoebe. Her voice sounded loud, and brought with it a rush of noise. Bea flapped her hand at her urgently, then poked her finger in her free ear.

"What am I doing?" she said to Theo.

Theo sighed patiently. "You're sitting on the branch beside me. You've got your finger stuck in your ear. You're listening to a jam jar through a thingie. Are you going to ask me why next?"

"Why?" repeated Bea.

"I haven't a clue," said Theo. "Did you bring Nails?"

"Nails is fine," said Bea. She had not tried to put the meerkat back in the backpack. From the corner of her eye she could see him foraging for beetles in the long grass. Now that he had won his freedom in a daring escape he seemed content to stay close.

"You keep saying that," said Theo, "but where is he? I caught a big green thing for him, but it keeps trying to climb out of my pocket."

"Never mind that," said Bea.

"I do mind. What if it's got a stinger?"

"Theo, listen to me. I know this will sound strange, but . . ." She tried to think of a way to phrase what she had to say that would not alarm him. "You can see me, but I can only hear you. I'm not actually sitting on a branch; I'm sitting on a rock."

"No, you're not," said Theo. "The rock would fall out of the tree. Then you'd fall out of the tree. Then you'd cry, and I'd get the blame."

"No, it wouldn't fall, because . . . Look, just describe to me where you are. Pretend I'm blind."

"Okay," said Theo after a moment. "There's trees. Lots of them."

"What kind of trees?"

"Skinny thin ones, mostly. They wave about a lot."

Bea looked into the forest through which they had just walked. The trees were old and sturdy there. Even the thinnest ones had trunks far thicker than a man's torso. "What else can you see?" she asked.

"Just a bunch of leaves. And the Tree People."

"What Tree People?"

"The ones who live here. They have tons of pets. They've got about a million cats, and a couple of lizards, and a big parrot called Trigger. . . ."

"Are they there now?" asked Bea.

"Of course," said Theo.

"Ask them where you are."

Theo's voice became muffled, as though he were talking away from the phone.

"We're Here."

"Where's here?" asked Bea. They were both talking now with that sort of exaggerated politeness people use when their patience has stretched to its limit.

"Just . . . Here," said Theo. "I think that's actually the name of it."

"Let me talk to them," said Bea.

"I'm not stopping you," said Theo.

"But I can't hear them," said Bea in exasperation.

"That's because they don't talk with voices."

Bea searched for a question that might produce an

answer that was of use to her. Her ear was numb from being pressed so hard against the flat end of the horn, and the strain of hearing his distant voice was making her dizzy. "What else can you see?" she said.

"I can see you and that stupid jar," said Theo. "I can see trees. I can see leaves; I can see the sky. It's nice here, but I want to go back to the busmarine now."

His voice seemed to be getting fainter as he grew more impatient. Bea could barely hear him, and in desperation she shouted one last question. "What color is the moon?"

The sound of the falls rushed into her ears like water breaching a dam, and if there was any reply from Theo she could not hear it. She called his name again, but there was no answer. She put the Squeak Jar down in the grass and ran her hands through her hair.

"Is he gone?" said Phoebe.

Bea nodded, trying to ignore the clammy feeling in her chest.

"Don't worry," said Phoebe. "Granny Delphine said you'd be able to find him when you've had some training."

"I don't think Ma will allow it. She's always hated Mumbo Jumbo."

"What *is* Mumbo Jumbo?"

"I don't know exactly. It's some kind of secret thing that Granny Delphine belongs to. We were always told never to mention it, ever. Ma says it's dangerous. Pa says it doesn't exist, but he says it in that voice he uses when he's making stuff up."

"Like when he told us a giant lizard runs the pizzeria?"

"Yes. Or about the chocolate mines of Kathmandu."

"Did he really think we'd believe those stories?"

Bea shrugged. "Would you have believed him if he had told us about a car wash that sent you to another world?"

Phoebe poked in the grass with a twig. For a while she said nothing; then she looked up at Bea. "You know what this place is, don't you?" she asked.

"What do you mean?"

"Bell Hoot is an anagram. Think about it."

Bea scratched her head. "Boot Hell?" she said. "Tell Hobo?" She knew she wasn't nearly as good at this as Phoebe was.

"No," said Phoebe. "I reckon it's a bolt-hole."

"What's a bolt-hole?"

"It's where people go to hide. It comes from rabbits, I think. This must be where people come to hide when the Gummint men are after them."

"Do you think we'll ever get back?" said Bea. She had been too concerned with Theo's disappearance during the short time they had spent in Bell Hoot to think about much else. Now for the first time it occurred to her that Phoebe might never see her parents again. She pictured Phoebe's dressing-gowned mother, her straw-colored hair showing two inches of gray roots and a cigarette glued to her mouth with scarlet lipstick, and the father who lurked in the sitting room with the curtains drawn, oblivious to anyone who was not holding a fistful of playing cards. Phoebe seldom mentioned her parents, and she certainly seemed to prefer the bustle and chaos of the Flints' apartment to the smoky cave of her own. "Will they be worried?" said Bea. "Your parents, I mean."

"They won't even notice I'm gone, probably," said Phoebe.

"Still," said Bea, "I don't see why you couldn't go back sometime if you wanted to."

"I don't want to," said Phoebe, concentrating on the small crater she had dug with the twig. "And I can't. You heard what the captain said. There's always seven more coming through."

"Yes, but if Bontoc arranged it in advance, maybe

they could bring through one person less."

Phoebe got to her feet. "If I did want to," she said, pointing at the opened compartment in the Blue Moon Mobile, "I could just stow away."

"I think that would still count as—," began Bea; then she stopped dead. A terrible thought struck her. She stared at Phoebe.

"What?" said Phoebe.

"I thought it was Nails who made Theo disappear," said Bea.

She saw her friend's eyes widen with the same realization.

"Arkadi!" they whispered in unison.

# Arkadi

**B**ea Flint and Phoebe Lu hurried back along the path toward Bell Hoot, while Nails the meerkat dozed happily in the jogging darkness of the backpack, his belly full of worms and beetles. The pale ghost of a blue moon remained in the sky. Below it the dawn had begun to spread on the western horizon—a fact that would have seemed strange to the two girls if they had had a compass to point it out to them. They were discussing whether they should tell anyone about the mysterious stowaway on the Blue Moon Mobile.

"We did promise him," said Phoebe.

"I know, but why was he so worried? Do you think he knows that someone has disappeared because he was there?" Now that they had left the falls behind, Bea could hear again the warm humming she had noticed earlier. She wondered vaguely what it could be.

"We don't know that for sure ourselves. And he doesn't seem very bright," said Phoebe, her arms stretched out for balance as she walked along a narrow log by the path's edge.

"I don't think he's as simple as he'd like us to believe. How did he get out of that compartment?"

"Didn't you let him out?"

"No. He unscrewed the panel from inside. How can you undo screws from the pointed end?"

They passed the stone library. The windows were dark, overlooking the square like empty eye sockets. The path that led to the Millers' house seemed unnaturally silent now.

"He did have a tool belt," said Phoebe. "And anyway, we don't know what they'll do to him if we tell. Maybe they burn people at the stake here."

"I doubt it," said Bea. She chewed her lip. "But you're right. We should find out some more. We'll bring him some food later, and see if we can—"

"Bea—" Phoebe interrupted her quietly. She pointed along the path. An eerie scene was unfolding in the cobwebby shadows. A strange mob of people surrounded the Millers' house. They all had similar features—broad, flat faces and round staring eyes. Their clothes were worn and patched. Most wore fingerless gloves and some had scarves wrapped around their heads like desert nomads, despite the warmth of the night. Their hair—where it could be seen—was long and tangled. It was not their appearance, however, that made Bea stop in her tracks. They seemed to be performing a bizarre circus act. The sturdier members of the group stood just outside the circle of thornbushes that was planted beneath the house. Others had climbed onto their shoulders, and as Bea and Phoebe watched in dreadful fascination a third group of these odd intruders was clambering up to stand on the shoulders of the second. The whole operation was carried out in deathly silence.

Bea reached out to grab Phoebe's arm and pull her out of sight among the bushes, but Phoebe had other ideas. She was already marching along the center of the path and into the small clearing in front of the house. The third wave was just reaching the high windows of the Millers' house when Phoebe spoke up.

"What do you think you're doing?" she said in a loud voice. Several of the intruders jumped visibly, and one of their human towers collapsed, pitching the boy

who made up its third tier into the thornbushes. He
was about twelve, and he let out a yelp as the thorns bit
him. It was the first sound that any of them had made,
and as the boy struggled to extract himself from the
thornbush Bea could see he was biting his lip to avoid
making another. She forced herself to follow Phoebe,
wishing she could be half as fearless as her friend.

An ancient, squat woman appeared from the far
side of the house. She said nothing, but the rest of
the mob quickly dismounted as though she had given
an invisible signal. The woman had the flat face and
widely spaced, almost colorless eyes of her clan. It was
the paleness of the eyes in particular that gave her
stare such an unnerving intensity. Her hair was tied
behind her head in a tight bun and she had a thin scarf
wrapped several times around her neck. She walked
silently up to where Bea and Phoebe stood, and looked
at each of them in turn. Bea found it hard to meet her
gaze, and even Phoebe's defiant stare seemed to wilt
a little. The woman spoke in a voice like a rusty nail.
"You're new here," she croaked. "Who came with
you?"

"Captain Bontoc," said Bea. She knew this was not
what the old woman was asking, but she felt compelled

to give an answer, and she hoped that this one would give nothing away.

"Fool," spat the old woman. It was not clear whether she was referring to Bea or to the captain. "Any more children?"

"No," said Phoebe, which was at least half true. "What were you doing at the windows of the Millers' house?"

The woman glared at her. "Neighborhood watch," she said. She looked from one to the other again. Bea felt exposed under her gaze, as if she were in the middle of a field in a thunderstorm, wearing only her underwear.

At that moment the Millers' front door swung open and Mr. Miller's voice called, "Who's there?" through the gloom.

The intruders vanished in a moment. As Bea watched they simply slid away between the trees, all except the old lady and the boy, who was extracting himself from the thornbush, and disappeared from view.

The old woman leaned closer, until her nose almost touched Bea's and her eyes seemed to merge into one pale disk with a black hole in the center. She smelled strongly of mothballs. "There's more," she croaked quietly. She turned and strode silently past the house. "Ike," she said in a low voice as she passed the boy in the thornbush. Ike freed himself with a final push. He ran clumsily after the gray-haired woman, and Bea thought she heard her say, "Idiot boy!" as they slipped away among the trees.

# Tattoo

"Couldn't sleep, eh?" said Mr. Miller, leaning over the rail of the verandah. He turned his head and said, "Ladder," and this time the ladder unfolded itself smartly, aided by a sharp tap from Mr. Miller's foot. Bea and Phoebe climbed the ladder and sank onto two of the cane chairs. "You can join me for breakfast," said Mr. Miller. "I like to make an early start."

He disappeared into the living room and came out a few moments later with a large breakfast tray. The eggs and toast scattered themselves onto plates in a considerably less tidy way than Mrs. Miller had managed the night before. "Oops," said Mr. Miller. He poured the coffee by hand.

"Plumegranates," said Mrs. Miller, appearing on the verandah in a silk dressing gown. She carried a bowl of fat red fruit. "Try them. Very sweet."

Bea took a bite of the strange fruit. It tasted like raspberries and honey, with a hint of marzipan.

"There were some strange people trying to look in through your windows when we came back," she said, wiping juice from her chin. She was carrying too many secrets already, and she was sure this was something their hosts should know.

Mrs. Miller put down the bowl with a clatter. Her hand flew to her mouth and she looked at her husband with wide eyes. "The *Ledbetters*!" she said.

"Did you leave the back ladder down when you went out?" said Mr. Miller sharply.

Bea shook her head. "Phoebe pulled the ladder back up, and then jumped down."

"They were standing on one another's shoulders," said Phoebe with admiration. "They were pretty good at balancing."

"They said they were neighborhood watch," added Bea.

"Which windows?" asked Mr. Miller.

"I don't think they reached any of them," said Bea. "They would have had to lean in over the bushes, and Phoebe stopped them before they got high enough."

Mr. Miller took a long slurp of his coffee and eyed them from the caves beneath his eyebrows. "You're sure they didn't reach the windows?" he said.

"As sure as I can be," said Bea.

"Who are the Ledbetters?" asked Phoebe. "What were they after?"

The Millers looked at each other. "They need to know," said Mrs. Miller.

Mr. Miller cleared his throat. He took a large bite from a slice of toast and munched on it for a while to give himself time to think.

"Before Willow gets up," said his wife gently.

"The Ledbetters are the oldest clan in Bell Hoot," Mr. Miller said through a mouthful of toast. "They live on a small island in the middle of Mumpfish Lake, about three miles from here. There used to be fruit trees on the island, but they cut them down for firewood many years ago."

"That doesn't sound very smart," said Bea.

"They left nothing growing on the island, not even heather. Nobody knows why they did it. Their clan leader is old Maize Ledbetter. She was very highly regarded at one time, but she became more eccentric as she got older. Some believe she's as crazy as a hen, but she's also a very shrewd woman, and gifted with second sight. She has predicted many things with great accuracy." He took another sip of coffee. "You may be sure she had a good reason for chopping the trees down, at least in her own mind. Now they grow nothing on the island, and scrape a living from farm laboring and odd jobs on the mainland."

"And burglary," said Mrs. Miller.

"And burglary," echoed Mr. Miller. "That was bad enough, but recently things took a turn for the worse. It's not valuables they're after anymore." He buttered another slice of toast thoughtfully, searching for the words he needed.

"Aren't the police able to stop them?" asked Phoebe, who was only half listening.

"We don't have police here," said Mrs. Miller. "Bell Hoot is a small enough place. Everyone knows everyone else, at least by sight. People get along most of the time, and when disputes arise they can usually be settled by the Quorum."

"What's the Quorum?" asked Bea.

"It's where I'm going this morning," said Granny Delphine, emerging from the dining room. She was dressed all in black and looked like she meant business.

"I think you have to put yourself on the agenda first," said Mrs. Miller. "There's usually a couple of weeks to wait."

Granny Delphine turned her spotlight stare on Mrs. Miller, smiled politely, and sat down to breakfast. "Is that coffee? I would love a cup of tea, if you don't mind."

Mrs. Miller picked up the same pot from which her husband had poured the coffee. "Tea," she said, and poured a cup of steaming red tea.

"Thank you," said Granny Delphine. "I'm sure the Quorum will regard my grandson's disappearance as a matter of urgency." She turned to Bea. "The Quorum is a sort of town council, except that I believe they actually get things done. I am going there this morning to see if I can find someone who can be of help."

"I spoke to Theo again," said Bea, "through the Squeak Jar."

"What did he say?" asked Granny Delphine.

"I asked him to describe where he was," said Bea. "He said it's a place with thin trees, and there's always a breeze."

"Where might that be, Mr. Miller?" said Granny Delphine.

Mr. Miller scratched the back of his head. "Thin

trees," he said. "Nowhere around here. This forest is old, and the trees are massive, as you can see."

"That sounds like the perfect opportunity for the two of you to do some exploring," said Granny Delphine to Bea and Phoebe. She turned around at a sound from the living room. "And this must be Willow," she said. "Maybe she'd like to go with you."

A young girl drifted out onto the verandah. She looked like a thinner version of her mother, but unlike Mrs. Miller's porcelain skin, Willow's complexion was pale and clammy, like cheese soaked in water. She walked as if in a dream, and barely glanced at Bea and Phoebe. She picked up a plumegranate without sitting down.

"I don't think so," said Mrs. Miller. "Willow hasn't been well. She gets tired easily."

"I get tired easily," said Willow in a flat voice. She stared out into the trees without eating the fruit in her hand.

"You were telling us about the Ledbetters," said Phoebe, to break the silence.

Mrs. Miller cleared her throat, and Mr. Miller stood up abruptly. "Nothing more to tell," he said, without meeting Phoebe's eye. It was obvious the subject was closed for now. He turned to Granny Delphine.

"The Quorum starts early. I'll point you in the right direction."

Mrs. Miller began to clear up the breakfast dishes noisily, as her husband and Granny Delphine descended the ladder. "Another plumegranate? I'll make you some sandwiches. It looks like rain later. Were the beds comfortable? You could take the old road past the orchards. You'll pass the windmill and turn left. There are copses of younger trees there. Don't know if any of them are big enough to get lost in, mind. You girls will need some sleep before you go."

"I'm not tired," said Bea.

"Me neither," said Phoebe. "I want to go exploring now."

"Well, if you're sure," said Mrs. Miller, "I'll go and make you some lunch to bring." She picked up the breakfast tray. "Willow," she said gently. "Willow?" The thin girl started, and turned to them as if trying to remember where she was. "This is Bea and this is Phoebe. They'll be staying with us for a while. Why don't you sit down?" said Mrs. Miller. She swept into the kitchen, leaving the three girls alone.

Willow sagged into a chair and looked at them with dull eyes. "You're new," she said.

"We arrived last night," said Bea.

"I heard you," said Willow.

"Did we wake you up?" asked Phoebe.

Willow shook her head. "I don't sleep," she said.

At that moment the tree house began to vibrate with heavy thumping. Even in a strange house Bea recognized it immediately as the sound of Pa descending the stairs. His voice boomed from inside. "I don't see the harm in asking. I can't just sit here all day."

"What are you going to do?" replied Ma's voice. "Go around the town asking, 'Have you seen a boy?'"

"I can describe him," said Pa, as he loomed onto the verandah. "Morning, girls."

"Describe him, then," said Ma.

"Well, he's . . ." A frown crossed his face. "Is he six or seven?"

"That's a good start," said Ma. "Bea, have you even brushed your hair since we left the apartment?" She sat down and smiled briefly at Willow.

"Seven years old, brownish hair. Well, lightish. Front teeth missing, face probably dirty," said Pa, counting off details on his thick fingers.

"We don't even have a photograph," said Ma.

"I'll just have to do without," said Pa. "Either way, I can't just sit around doing nothing."

Bea could hear the background hum she had noticed

the night before: It was stronger now in the daylight, and it reminded her of a sound she remembered from years before. Her mother had still had her tattoo parlor back then, before Theo was born. Bea could remember sitting in the overstuffed armchair, watching Ma trace the curving tendrils of a climbing rose or adding the heat to a dragon's flaming breath, working so quickly that the picture would spread across the customer's skin like spilled ink. She could still see the contentment on her mother's face as she worked, and hear the sound of her tattoo machine buzzing reassuringly in the corner. She looked at Ma now. There were dark rings under her eyes, and she was shredding a tissue between her fingers.

A sudden thought struck Bea. "You could tattoo a picture of him, Ma!" she said. "Then Pa would be able to show it to everyone."

Pa looked at her with admiration. "That's a genius idea!" He laid his forearm on the table and turned it over, pale side up like a fish's belly. "I've still got a gap right here, between the tiger's head and the butterfly in boots."

"And what would I use for equipment?" said Ma.

Pa guffawed. "You can't fool me," he said. "I could

feel the weight of it in your suitcase. You always bring it on holiday."

"Then when you get home you always put it back in the cupboard and say, 'I don't know why I brought this stuff,'" said Bea.

"I haven't done a tattoo in years," said Ma doubtfully, but Bea could see the ghost of a smile through the sorrow on her face.

"Won't make a bit of difference," said Pa. "You were the best in the business, and it will all come back to you the moment the ink hits the skin. Isn't that right, Bea?"

But Bea had already gone, through the dining room and up the stairs to fetch the honey-colored wooden tattoo box from her mother's suitcase.

# Bees

**B**ea Flint and Phoebe Lu walked along the forest path in the direction Mrs. Miller had indicated. They intended to double back as soon as they could find a turnoff. Bea had put their sandwiches in the outer pocket of Theo's backpack to protect them from the hungry meerkat. She would give the sandwiches to Arkadi, and in return she had questions to ask him. The buzzing from Ma's tattoo machine faded slowly into the background hum of the forest. A fat bumblebee sailed past them, and suddenly Bea realized what the sound was. "Bees!" she said.

"What about them?" said Phoebe.

"That's what that humming sound is."

"I can't hear anything."

"You can't?" said Bea. She spread her arms wide.

"It's all around us. I could hear it in the night too, but not as loud."

"There's a turn here," said Phoebe. They took a sharp right. After a short while the path began to curve back on itself, and they could see the back of the library building through the trees. "This must be the other path that goes to Cambio Falls," said Phoebe. "I think I'll be able to find the hut when we get closer."

They left the path after a while and made their way through the trees, clambering over twisted roots. Brightly colored birds perched just above their heads, eyeing them with black button eyes. A snake broke cover just in front of them and disappeared again into the shivering under-growth. Bea kept her eyes peeled for monkeys.

They stumbled across the hut by accident. It was a tiny dilapidated wooden building, almost invisible among the trees. The roof was made from dried branches, which Arkadi seemed to have supplemented in the night with newer greenery. He sat outside the hut, whittling a stick with a knife. He looked up and smiled.

"Hello," said Bea.

"I heard you coming," said Arkadi. "You make enough noise for nine sumo wrestlers."

"We brought you some sandwiches."

"Did you steal them?"

"They were made for us, but we've already eaten."

Arkadi unwrapped a sandwich and took a bite so enormous that he could hardly chew it. From his throat came a muffled sound that might have been, "Thank you."

Bea seated herself on a log and waited patiently. Phoebe began to climb the nearest tree. Arkadi gave a grunt and wagged his finger at her. He swallowed noisily. "Don't climb," he said. "Ringsnakes in these trees. They'll kill you stone dead and you'll fall, bump, bang, crack. Break every bone in your body and they'll have to bury you in a cake tin."

"Ringsnakes?" said Phoebe.

"Ringsnakes," said Arkadi. "They sit like a ring around the trunk. You can't avoid them whichever side you climb."

"I thought you'd never been here before," said Phoebe.

"I haven't," said Arkadi. "Heard many, many stories, though."

"Have you heard of a clan called the Ledbetters?" said Bea.

"Bedwetters?" said Arkadi. He looked at Bea with

an open face. It gave nothing away.

"Ledbetters," said Phoebe, jumping to the ground from a high branch. "They look in through people's windows at night."

"What are they looking for?" said Arkadi.

"We don't know," said Bea. "But the family we're staying with seems frightened of them."

"There are always things to be afraid of," said Arkadi. "It's what you do about them that matters."

"Like hiding in a hut?" said Bea.

"I'm just hiding till I figure out what's best."

"What will they do if they find you?"

"They won't find me," said Arkadi. "I'm good at hiding."

"And if we tell?" said Bea.

"You promised."

"My little brother disappeared on the crossing," said Bea. "Captain Bontoc says that's never happened before."

Arkadi glanced up from his stick. "I'm sorry to hear that. Little brothers are hard to replace."

"Do you think he disappeared because you were under the floor?" said Bea.

"Why would he do that?" said Arkadi.

"'Sky black, moon blue, nine souls go through,'" said Phoebe. "It says it on the side of the Blue Moon Mobile."

"That's just a slogan," said Arkadi. "Like 'Men's shirts three for two on Tuesdays,' or 'Half a dozen is better than six of . . .'" He put down his knife and his stick and began to count on his fingers. He looked confused. "I was never good with phrases," he said. "I'm good at fixing things. That's me. And hiding," he added.

"How did you unscrew the panel from the inside?" said Bea.

"That's another thing I'm good at," said Arkadi, "unscrewing things from the inside." He picked up his stick again, and Bea could see he was carving it into the shape of a meerkat. "Thank you for the sandwiches," he said, without looking up.

# Fire

"He didn't seem to know anything about Theo," said Phoebe. They had retraced their steps and were following the path that Mrs. Miller had first suggested. They passed the plumegranate orchards, where a dozen pickers were working, loading the ripe fruit into a large handcart that Mr. Miller wheeled between the trees. He waved at them as they passed.

"I'm not so sure," said Bea, waving back. "I think he was just avoiding our questions."

"If he doesn't want to tell us more, I don't see how we can make him."

"We can still threaten to turn him in."

"But we promised."

Bea stopped in the road. "Granny Delphine always says, 'Blood is thicker than water.'" She knelt down and unzipped the backpack. Nails poked his nose out and sniffed, then jumped out gratefully and scurried to the grass verge to forage for his breakfast.

"What does that mean?"

"I think it means that your family is more important than anything. If I thought it would help us to find Theo I wouldn't think twice about turning Arkadi in."

They passed a slightly ramshackle windmill and turned left, walking on through the open countryside in the gathering heat. Bea noticed that she could hear different notes in the buzzing of the bees. Not only could she tell how near they were and in what numbers, but before long she could distinguish the bees of one hive from those of another. When she mentioned this to Phoebe she found to her surprise that Phoebe could hear only a bee that was flying close. She could not hear the network of bees crisscrossing the fields as Bea could, nor the hum of distant hives.

Ahead of them the road curved through a range of low rounded hills. They could see three or four small copses of trees, their trunks slender and their leaves pale and feathery in the distance. Nails had stayed close, as she thought he would. He trotted along on the road ahead, sometimes diving into a ditch to rummage in the long grass, then running to catch up. Bea could feel a knot forming in her stomach. She pictured Theo sitting there among the trees, waiting impatiently for her to arrive. She did not want to get her hopes up, and she pushed the picture from her mind.

"Do you think that might be where he is?" said Phoebe.

"I hope so," said Bea, "but things aren't usually that simple." She concentrated on the sound of the bees to keep her mind occupied. Reaching the trees seemed to be taking forever. She noticed that the tracks of the bees were converging on the nearest copse. A fat honeybee arrowed past them, but as it approached the copse it began to zigzag and fly in circles.

"I wish we hadn't given away all our sandwiches," said Phoebe.

Bea smiled. "It doesn't matter," she said. "We'll have honey instead."

"Did we bring honey?"

"No, but there's a hive in those trees."

"How do you know?"

"That bee told me," said Bea. "It flies straight toward home, but when it gets near the hive it flies in circles."

"Maybe it's lost."

Bea shook her head. "I think it's trying to confuse us, so we can't easily spot the hive."

"You never went around in circles when you got near your apartment."

"I'm not a bee," said Bea. "Not a honeybee, anyway," she corrected herself.

They had reached the trees now. There were about twenty of them, tall and slender with silver bark and heart-shaped leaves. Bea stood for a while, her eyes closed and her ears open to the pattern of bee trails that surrounded her. "There," she said, and she opened her eyes. She pointed to a hole in the trunk of a tree a little way ahead of them. A couple of bees were coming in to land, and more were setting out on foraging duty.

Phoebe shaded her eyes and looked. "I can see them now," she said, "but how will we get the honey?"

Bea put Theo's backpack at the foot of the tree. "First we've got to look for Theo," she said. The trees were spaced far enough apart for grass to grow beneath them, dappled by the sunlight through the leaves. It did not seem likely that even a small boy could be easily hidden here. Bea took the Squeak Jar from the backpack. She sat down in the cool grass and placed the listening horn to the lid. "Theo?" she said.

"What?" said Theo's voice. There was no waterfall to mask the sound now, and she could hear him clearly. He sounded quite cheerful.

"You never answered me about the moon," said Bea.

"What about it?"

"Is it blue or yellow?"

"How should I know? It's the middle of the day."

"Are the Tree People there?"

"They're always here."

"Ask them why they're keeping you."

There was a brief conversation, though Bea could make out only Theo's muffled voice. "They're just looking after me. They said I've always been here."

"But you just got there yesterday," said Bea.

"The Tree People have never heard of yesterday," said Theo.

"What do you mean?"

"I don't know. It's funny. They only remember what's happened since we woke up this morning, but they know lots of stuff."

Bea shook her head as if to clear it. This didn't seem to be getting her any closer to finding Theo.

"Can you still see me?" she asked him.

"I can when you're here," said Theo.

"Pinch my arm," said Bea.

"But you're always telling me not to do that."

"This time I want you to."

"You'll just pinch me back," said Theo with a touch of suspicion.

"I can't even see you," said Bea. She tried to keep the impatience from her voice. She waited, but nothing happened.

"What now?" came Theo's voice.

"I didn't feel anything."

"That was my best pinch," said Theo indignantly. "The twisty one. Usually you scream like those peacocks in the zoo."

Bea gave a short laugh. She wished more than anything that Theo were right there with her and Phoebe. She wouldn't mind how much he was annoying her. "I just wish you could tell me where you are," she said.

"The Tree People say that a wish is no good unless you can give it legs," said Theo.

"How can a wish have legs?" asked Bea.

"Beats me," said Theo. "They say lots of weird things."

Bea looked around her in frustration. She was sure Theo couldn't be in the small copse where she and Phoebe sat. There were others scattered among the low hills, but it would take days to search them all.

If only there were a quicker way to find out if Theo was there.

"Can't you light a fire or something?" asked Bea, thinking of lost people on desert islands.

"Okay!" said Theo. "There's a magnifying glass on my penknife. If I can just get this dry leaf to stay still . . ." He sounded enthusiastic, and Bea thought about how he had set fire to the kitchen bin the year before. And the balcony, when he had been burning a picture onto a piece of wood with the same magnifying glass. And the bathroom, she remembered suddenly. How could *anyone* set fire to a bathroom?

"On second thought—," she began to say, but before she had finished there was a commotion from the Squeak Jar.

She heard Theo say, "Ouch! I didn't . . ." His voice became muffled. She called his name a couple of times, and just when she was about to give up, she heard him again faintly. "Have to go!" he said, and then there was silence.

 Quorum

**B**ea Flint inched her way up the trunk of the honey tree. The silvery bark was rough on her arms and her bare feet, but she was concentrating on the song of the bees and she barely noticed the discomfort. Above her the guard drones swarmed like black dots against the sky, and their humming rose to a higher pitch as they watched her approach the hive.

Bea hummed back to reassure them. *I won't hurt you,* was what she hoped her hum would say, *and I won't take all your honey.*

The humming of the bees seemed to calm a little. They began to land on her face and arms. She moved as slowly and carefully as she could, hugging the slender trunk like a koala. The bees' feet tickled her gently, but she felt no sting.

"Watch out for ringsnakes," whispered Phoebe from

below. She had wanted to be the one to climb the tree, but Bea had insisted. She didn't answer Phoebe now. There were bees crawling across her lips. She breathed as shallowly as she could for fear of sucking them up her nose. Her eyes were just open enough to allow her to see, though she felt sure she could navigate by the sound alone.

When she reached the hive she paused and tried to figure out how she could remove the honey and climb back down with only two hands. *I should have brought a bag*, she thought. She shifted her grip and reached into the hole with her right hand, as slowly as honey pouring. She could just see the honeycombs hanging in sheets inside the hive. She grasped the edge of a comb and pulled gently. The buzzing grew stronger. The bees sounded angry now, but Bea kept up her own quiet hum as she lifted the honeycomb slowly from the hive. She held it out at arm's length and squinted at it through half-closed eyes. *You can spare this one for us*, she hummed.

To her surprise the bees that crawled over it began to leave one by one, as though accepting that this honeycomb had changed owners. She dropped it into the long grass at Phoebe's feet. She wondered if she could make the bees leave her head and arms also. She was not afraid they would sting her—more that she might crush some of them as she inched back down the trunk. She hummed a thank-you to the bees, and felt the lightness as they took off like a fuzzy cloud and began to stream back into the tree. She climbed slowly down. Her arms and legs ached suddenly, and she almost fell from the tree before she reached the ground.

Phoebe was staring at her, openmouthed. "That was amazing!" she said. "One minute you looked like . . . like a giant bee lollipop; then you hummed at them and they just went 'poof!' You never told me you could do that."

"I didn't know myself," said Bea. "It just seemed like they returned to the hive when I asked them to." She picked up the honeycomb and turned it over to make sure there were no bees still on it. She took a bite. It tasted like nothing she had ever tasted before. A warm feeling spread through her. It felt like getting a generous gift from a distant relative you never knew you had.

They began the long walk home licking their fingers. The girls were sticky inside and out. The honey seemed to have gotten everywhere, even on the back of Phoebe's hair and on the soles of Bea's feet. Nails had shared the feast, and now lay in the warm darkness of the backpack, occasionally licking a paw in his sleep.

The plumegranate orchards were deserted by the time they passed them in the late afternoon. The hand-cart stood in a corner of the field, stacked high with empty picking baskets, and bees worked quietly among the wildflowers that grew between the trees. The path led them on into the forest, and in the cool shade of the ancient trees they sat down to drink the last of the water Mrs. Miller had given them and to rest their tired feet.

"I always thought Clockwork Gabby was mute," said Phoebe, tossing pebbles at a large mushroom that grew from the bark of a nearby tree.

"Granny Delphine didn't think so," said Bea. "She told me once that she thought Gabby had suffered a terrible shock, but she could never find out what it was."

"I wonder why she's started to speak now," said Phoebe.

Bea shrugged. "Maybe she feels safer here," she said. "Maybe it's a bolt-hole for her too. I'm not sure she's making sense, though."

"She said 'boygone,'" said Phoebe.

"That's easy enough," said Bea, "but she said something else before that, when we were walking up from the falls. It sounded like *beanos*."

"What are beanos?"

"I don't know."

"Did you wind her up this morning?" asked Phoebe.

Bea shook her head. "I'm sure Ma did. She never forgets."

"I hope so," said Phoebe. She picked up a larger stone and knocked the mushroom clean off the trunk. "What do you suppose is wrong with Willow?" she said.

"Whatever it is, it has something to do with the Ledbetters. The Millers didn't want to discuss them anymore once she appeared."

"The Ledbetters don't look sick. They look weird, though. Maybe they scared her half to death, climbing up the walls like that."

She picked up the mushroom she had dislodged and began to pick it apart with her nails. Bea closed her eyes and tuned in again to the network of bees that was working among the trees. They were fewer and more spread out here in the woods than out in the open. There weren't as many flowers in the shade, Bea supposed. By concentrating hard on the sound of the bees she could make a sort of map of her surroundings in her mind's eye. She could hear in the distance a few busier spots, not busy enough to be hives, which she guessed must be small clearings where flowers grew. She could tell where the larger trees were, because the bees had to fly in a wide circle around them. One of the trees in her sound map seemed to be moving. *That can't be right*, she thought, and she opened her eyes.

It was not a moving tree that the bees were circling, but a squat woman with her hair in a bun, gliding swiftly through the shadows. She wore a scarf and gloves as before, and Bea wondered how she could stand to be so wrapped up in the heat. She nudged Phoebe in the ribs. "Sssssh!" she said, before Phoebe had a chance to speak. She pointed into the trees on the far side of the path. "It's that Ledbetter woman," she whispered. "The one who said she was the neighborhood watch."

"What's she up to?" said Phoebe.

The woman was frowning and muttering to herself. She walked quickly through the undergrowth, following no visible path, but still she did not make a sound.

"Don't leap up and ask her," whispered Bea. "Let's see where she goes."

They sat quietly on the pathside, waiting for the woman to get far enough away that they could follow her without being seen. To their surprise she took a sudden turn to face an enormous oak tree. The trunk of the tree was so thick that twenty people with linked hands could not have encircled it. A broad crack ran up from the roots to just below the lowest branches. Higher up the trunk Bea noticed what appeared to be windows cut here and there in the rough bark. The woman exchanged a few words with someone they could not see. She stepped through the crack and disappeared into the darkness.

The two girls stared at each other in surprise. "I thought she lived on an island," said Phoebe.

"Maybe she's visiting someone."

"Let's take a closer look," said Phoebe.

Bea put the empty canteen into the backpack, being careful not to let Nails escape. They crossed the path and crept in among the trees. As they got closer they could see a man sitting on one of the oak tree's enormous roots. He had a wedge-shaped head and large dark eyes. His thinning hair was slicked across the top of his head. He reminded Bea of the grasshopper who had selected Mr. Miller to be their host. His head was nodding with sleep, but every now and then he jerked himself awake and peered blearily about.

"We need to distract him somehow," whispered Phoebe.

"It looks like he'll fall asleep before long," said Bea.

"That could take forever. She might come out again anytime."

An idea came to Bea, and she smiled to herself. She began to hum very quietly, the way she had done to calm the bees before taking their honey. Phoebe gave her a puzzled look, but Bea put her finger to her lips and kept humming. The doorman's head nodded again. This time his chin settled firmly on his chest, and within a short time he had begun to snore.

"How did you do that?" asked Phoebe, stifling a yawn herself.

"I'm not sure," whispered Bea. "I tried to make the sound bees make when they don't sense any danger. Maybe we all know that sound in the back of our minds, without realizing it."

"I don't remember ever seeing a bee till we got here," said Phoebe.

"We need to find a way in," said Bea. "We can't go through the front door in case we meet her coming out."

"We can climb up the far side and look in through the windows."

Bea snorted with laughter. She put her hand over her mouth and checked on the doorman. He was still fast asleep. "Like the neighborhood watch," she whispered, but Phoebe was already walking silently toward the tree. She stooped to pick a bright yellow flower, and creeping straight up to the sleeping doorman she tucked it gently behind his ear. Bea held her breath, but the man slept on.

The mighty roots of the oak tree swept up from the forest floor, making the first part of the climb easy. Bea and Phoebe had removed their shoes to make their progress quieter. Bea's stomach tightened with fear when she thought of the Ledbetter woman's menacing stare. What if the old woman looked out of one of the glassless windows just as they reached it?

There was a small round opening just below a branch, and she pointed silently to it. Phoebe nodded and ran up the steep trunk as though it were horizontal, waiting just below the window level for Bea to catch up.

They reached the window and peered cautiously inside. The tree was indeed completely hollow. A circular floor had been built about halfway up the inside of the trunk, some distance below the high window. There was a hole in the center of the floor. The top of a ladder could be seen poking up through it. Nine chairs were arranged in a circle around the walls of the chamber. All of them were occupied. The Ledbetter woman stood by the top of the ladder with her hands on her hips, glaring at the person sitting in the chair in front of her. As Bea's eyes got used to the dimness she saw with a start that the occupant of the chair was none other than Granny Delphine.

"Then you must be Maize Ledbetter," her grandmother was saying. "I've heard all about you."

"You'll have heard a pack of lies, then," said the woman in her scratchy voice. "And you're sitting in my chair."

"Mrs. Walker arrived unexpectedly," said a man with a wispy beard from the far side of the chamber. "She had an urgent matter to put before us."

Bea looked at Phoebe and silently mouthed the word *Quorum*. Phoebe nodded.

"In any case we weren't expecting you . . . ," began a beefy man who sat beside Granny Delphine. He looked as though he could wrestle a bull with one hand while enjoying a pint of turpentine with the other, but he sounded nervous speaking to the flat-faced woman.

Maize Ledbetter snorted. "Nine clan leaders are entitled to sit in the Quorum, no more. I turns up when I sees fit. Between times my chair stays empty.

Newcomers always think their little complaints is urgent." She turned back to Granny Delphine. "What is it, then—Millers' beds got fleas? Lost your post office book?"

"I lost my grandson," said Granny Delphine, making no move to vacate Maize Ledbetter's chair. "Perhaps you have a suggestion as to where we might find him. I believe you've lived here longer than anyone."

The other woman started slightly at the mention of the lost grandson; then her expression became blank, as though a shutter had rolled down over her thoughts. "I've seen 'em all arrive," she said at length. "Arguing, complaining, crying for their lost hamsters. Never seen a bunch careless enough to lose a kid, mind you, not in all these years. A boy, you said?"

"A seven-year-old boy named Theo," said Granny Delphine. "Some of the council members seem to think you might know something about it."

Bea could tell which were the council members who had expressed this opinion. They cleared their throats and looked at the floor. They checked their finger-nails for dirt. They directed their eyes anywhere but at Maize Ledbetter.

"And why do they think that?" said Maize. There

was quiet menace in her tone. "They been complaining about nightmares again?"

"They say that members of your clan invade people's dreams while they sleep," said Granny Delphine. She stood up now, and fixed the other woman with a level stare. "And that in those dreams you say only one thing: 'Give us the Hidden Boy.'"

The two women stood motionless, face-to-face. Bea knew well the mesmerizing effect of her grandmother's stare, magnified as it was by her mysterious spectacles. She had been on the receiving end of Maize Ledbetter's cold glare as well. She thought about a mongoose facing a rattlesnake, and she watched with fascination to see which one would outstare the other.

"They all has nightmares," said Maize Ledbetter, "because of guilt. They keep us on a rock in the middle of a lake. Ain't nothing growing there. We got to slave for our keep. When that ain't enough we got to take what we need. No wonder they don't sleep easy."

"You chose to live on that island," said the man with the wispy beard, "and there were plenty of fruit trees on it once. You cut them all down."

"Who is the Hidden Boy?" interrupted Granny Delphine.

"You tell me," said Maize. She folded her arms. Neither woman had averted her gaze.

"My missing grandson can be heard, but not seen," said Granny Delphine. "Let's just suppose he is the Hidden Boy. What would you want with him?"

"Now, that's a different matter. If your boy do turn up, he must come to us. We got fostering rights."

"Fostering rights?" echoed Granny Delphine.

"Ask your new friends," said Maize Ledbetter. She looked away for a moment as she indicated the rest of the Quorum, and Bea felt that her grandmother had won a small victory.

Wispy Beard cleared his throat. "The eldest son of every newly arrived group is fostered to one of the nine clans for a year. It helps to forge ties and avoid . . . er . . . conflict."

"Tell her whose turn it is, Morganfield," said Maize.

"I can guess," said Granny Delphine, "but when we do find Theo you may be sure you won't be getting your hands on him."

Maize Ledbetter laughed. It was a dry croak that

you might expect to hear from a crow with laryngitis. "You don't have a choice," she said.

"She's right, I'm afraid," said Mr. Morganfield. "It's always been the rule, since Bell Hoot was founded."

"Rules are made to be broken," said Granny Delphine. Bea almost snorted. It was a notion that her grandmother had never allowed anyone else in the family to get away with.

"Not those that were given to us by Arkadi himself," said Mr. Morganfield.

Clinging to the outside of the tree, Bea and Phoebe looked at each other in puzzlement. Surely they couldn't be talking about the ice-cream mechanic who was hiding in the woods, whittling a meerkat from a stick?

"You have just arrived," Mr. Morganfield continued, "and I can understand that you are not familiar with the way things work here. Arkadi meant Bell Hoot to be a world that avoided the mistakes of the past. Every family that arrives here joins one of the nine clans. The Millers are part of the Morganfield clan, and so will you be, since they were chosen as your sponsors. As new arrivals your eldest male child must be fostered for one year to another clan, and it is the turn of the

Ledbetters to take him in. It's a finely tuned system, and it works. Every new family must abide by the rules. No exceptions."

A man stood up who had been sitting directly below the window through which the two girls were eavesdropping. They could see only his bald crown, fringed with gray hair. It looked like an ostrich egg in an untidy nest. The man spoke quietly. "My niece, Tilly Horton, died this morning." There was a shocked silence in the circular chamber. "She hadn't slept nor eaten for six months. There weren't nothing we could do for her. My sister's heart is torn asunder with grief." Bea felt the hair rising on the back of her neck.

"There's others in Bell Hoot that are fading fast," the man went on. "Little Erika Spivey, Jim Hooker, the Miller girl and more." The man raised a quivering finger and pointed at Maize Ledbetter. "It was her clan that killed my niece, sure as if they'd stuck a knife in her. I move that all rights be denied the Ledbetter clan. No fostering rights. No work. No handouts. Let them starve till they learn to act civilized."

Maize Ledbetter sneered at the speaker. It was an ugly expression on an already unpleasant face. "See what I mean? They gets a bellyache or a bad dream

and we gets the blame." She turned to Granny Delphine. "We'll get the boy. You'll see. Ledbetters don't
roll over for nobody."

She turned without another word and descended the
ladder. Bea and Phoebe flattened themselves against
the bark like geckos, so they did not see which way the
Ledbetter woman went.

# Maize

The meeting of the Quorum continued inside the great oak tree. Granny Delphine related Theo's description of his surroundings as Bea had told it to her, but none of the clan leaders could match it to any place they knew of. An agreement was reached that each clan would lend someone to help in the search. The discussion moved on to other topics, but talk of pest control and the price of turnips held no interest for Bea and Phoebe.

They crept quietly down the tree trunk and sat between two of the great roots, on the opposite side to the door. Bea frowned at the thought of Maize Ledbetter's determination to foster Theo for a year. It was unimaginable that once they finally found Theo they would have to hand him over to a surly gang of unwashed burglars.

They heard voices from the far side of the tree as

the clan heads left the Quorum and separated on the pathway. They could hear Granny Delphine stopping awhile to speak to the doorman. When they judged she had gone they stood up to leave.

Granny Delphine was standing on the other side of the root, her arms folded and a patient look on her face. "Are you quite ready?" she said.

Bea nodded sheepishly and shouldered Theo's backpack. Granny Delphine turned and began to march toward the path.

"How did you know we were here?" asked Phoebe, half running to keep up.

"I used my eyes," said Granny Delphine.

"I didn't see you look up once," said Phoebe.

"I didn't have to," said Granny Delphine. "When you looked through the window the light dimmed by just the amount that two children's heads would block, and the spiders and geckos on the far side of the chamber froze for a while, which meant someone was looking in their direction."

"But it could have been anyone," said Bea.

"Or a couple of monkeys," added Phoebe.

"I never heard of a monkey putting a flower behind the ear of a sleeping doorman," said Granny Delphine.

"Do you think anyone else knew we were there?" asked Bea.

"All of them, I would say," said Granny Delphine. "Mr. Morganfield has the hearing of a bat. They say he can hear grass growing on a stormy night, and your breathing would have been like two small hurricanes to him. Fred Horton would have felt through the soles of his feet the vibration as you climbed the trunk, and could probably tell your weight to the nearest ounce. You don't get to be head of a clan without a thorough grasp of Mumbo Jumbo."

"What *is* Mumbo Jumbo?" asked Bea.

"Your mother wouldn't want me to tell you," said Granny Delphine.

"But it's important, isn't it? Especially . . ." Bea chose her words carefully. "Especially with Theo gone."

"It has never been so important," agreed her grandmother. She looked at Bea with her owl eyes. "You're the one who can find Theo, but then, you will know that from listening to our conversation last night."

"Sorry," said Bea quietly.

"Sorry? For what, girl? You have already taken the first step toward a basic grasp of Mumbo Jumbo."

"Eavesdropping is the first step?"

Granny Delphine snorted. "Knowing what's going on is the first step. Manners are no good to you if they stop up your eyes and ears."

"Doesn't Mumbo Jumbo just mean *nonsense*?" asked Phoebe.

"It does," said Granny Delphine. "It was the Gummint who gave it that name, to try to weaken us with ridicule, but ridicule works only if you allow yourself to be offended. We adopted the term ourselves, and so it lost its teeth." She stopped suddenly in the middle of the path. "What do you know?" she said.

Bea looked about her, wondering what had surprised her grandmother. "What?" she said eventually.

"That was a question," said Granny Delphine. "What do you know?"

"I know lots of things," said Bea uncertainly.

"I'm not asking the square root of sixty-four or the capital of Belgium," said Granny Delphine. "What do you know right now? What are your senses telling you?"

Bea closed her eyes. "We're in a forest," she said. "I can hear the leaves rustling, so there's a breeze. There are lots of bees. . . ." She felt a little foolish mentioning things that seemed so obvious.

"Trees, breeze and bees," said Granny Delphine. "It's a start, but you've got a long way to go, child." She began walking again. "There are twenty-two different flowers growing a stone's throw from here. I'm not familiar with the Bell Hoot varieties, but there are five types of orchid, a kind of honeysuckle, something that might grow to resemble a melon, and two plants that eat insects, among others. One of those is trying to swallow a click beetle. I know that the doorman at the Quorum uses coconut butter on his hair and will be buying a new razor on Friday. That Ledbetter woman will send one of her clan to spy on the two of you wherever you go. It would be twenty-five past six if people used clocks here. It rained for three hours the night before we arrived in Bell Hoot." She turned and looked at Bea through her owl spectacles. "And you climbed a birch tree to raid a beehive this morning. Why you and not Phoebe? I would have thought that was more her department."

Bea's jaw dropped. It had always seemed that Granny Delphine had eyes in the back of her head, but how could she possibly know all these things?

"You're wondering how I could possibly know all these things," said her grandmother. "It's really very simple, but simple is not the same as easy. The meerkat in your backpack knows these things, because he pays attention to what his senses are telling him. All animals do, except for us. By the time we are thirteen we think we know what the world is about, so we stop paying attention."

"I think I can see how you would know about the flowers," said Bea, "but what about the rest?"

"The flowers announce themselves with perfume and color, of course. The sound of the click beetle is muffled, like he's being squeezed, and the doorman's hair smells of coconut. These are the easy parts."

"How do you know he'll buy a razor on Friday?" asked Bea.

"There was a small square of tissue stuck to the corner of his jaw, where he had nicked himself with a blunt razor. At the Quorum meeting it was agreed to pay him his wages on Friday. When I told him this he seemed relieved, and stroked his stubble with his fingers. I'm not certain he'll buy a razor with his pay, but I'd be happy to take a bet."

"What about the Ledbetter woman?"

"Maize Ledbetter passed this way after leaving the Quorum. She pushed through those bushes—see how that twig is broken, and the footprint beneath it?—but it was less than five minutes ago. I know this because she disturbed the bird who nests in that bush. You can see her circling overhead, and she hasn't returned to her nest yet."

"But Maize left the Quorum at least half an hour ago," said Phoebe.

"Precisely. That means she stayed nearby for some time after leaving. Since she already knew the kind of business the meeting would move on to, she must have stayed to eavesdrop on you two instead, but you didn't say anything that would be useful to her."

"How do you know we didn't?"

"Because you don't know where Theo is, and that's the information she wants. She probably suspects we've hidden him deliberately, so she'll send one of her grandchildren to shadow you. Once you know how to pay attention to the present, the future begins to come into sharper focus."

Bea shivered. "So even Maize Ledbetter knew we were there all along?"

Granny Delphine gripped Bea's elbow and stopped again in the path. "Maize Ledbetter is the oldest Pearlseed in Bell Hoot. It's said she knows the exact moment an apple will fall from the tree before it has started to grow." Her voice dropped to the softest whisper. "Maize was a student of Arkadi himself. He taught her everything she knows, and it was he who banished her to Bell Hoot."

"Who is Arkadi?" whispered Bea.

"He was the founder of Mumbo Jumbo," said Granny Delphine.

Bea wondered if Granny Delphine already knew they had hidden an ice-cream mechanic named Arkadi in the hut near Cambio Falls. She tried to keep her voice casual. "Is he still alive?" she asked.

Granny Delphine raised her eyebrows. "He was Maize Ledbetter's teacher when she was just a child. Maize herself is almost a hundred years old now."

Bea frowned. It seemed a strange sort of answer. "Doesn't anyone know for sure?" she said.

"He disappeared many years ago," said her grandmother. "Not even the Pearlseeds know what became of him, but I suspect he had a good reason for that."

"What is a Pearlseed?" asked Bea.

"You know how a pearl is formed, I suppose?" said Granny Delphine.

"A bit of grit gets into an oyster, and the pearl forms around it."

"Precisely so. The grit irritates the oyster, and in

protecting itself the oyster creates a thing of beauty."

"So a Pearlseed is an irritant."

"In a sense, yes. Sometimes it's necessary for people to be an irritant to society so that something more valuable might be born."

"Are you a Pearlseed?" asked Bea, but Granny Delphine put her finger to her lips and dropped her voice again.

"If you had learned anything from my introduction to Mumbo Jumbo you would know that your dinner is ready and your mother is almost within earshot," she said. "We will speak more about this later."

"But—," said Bea.

"No buts," said her grandmother firmly. She stopped at the edge of the path and pointed to a large white flower shaped like an inverted bell. "Three hours' rain," she said.

"How can you tell?" said Phoebe.

Granny Delphine flicked the flower, which sprinkled the surrounding leaves with a shower of water. "Any more than three hours and it would have tipped over and emptied itself out. Any less and it would not have been full."

"Maybe it did tip over, but it rained for six hours," said Bea.

"That's very good," said Granny Delphine. Bea felt herself flush with her grandmother's rare compliment. "But the ground would have been softer when we arrived," added Granny Delphine. "You'll find it was three."

As they approached the Millers' house they were met by an unexpected sight. The clearing was once again surrounded by people, but this time they were not trying to clamber up to the windows. Instead they formed a straggling line that stretched right around the house and disappeared among the trees. At the head of the line a man was sitting on a wooden stool. He was stripped to the waist, and Ma was perched on a bench behind him, frowning with concentration as she worked. Her buzzing needle flew back and forth with astonishing speed, tattooing across the man's back a lush forest that grew and curled and blossomed with color even as they watched. On the bench beside Ma sat Clockwork Gabby, whom Ma evidently had remembered to wind up. Gabby's eyes were fixed on the tattoo, and she handed Ma inks, tissues and needles with the speed and precision of a robot on an assembly line.

The people at the head of the line were bunched up around them, transfixed by the spreading riot of color, while those farther back craned just to catch a glimpse, but Ma seemed unaware of their presence. Bea could see that her mother was lost in the world that she was creating, and so contented did she look that Bea tiptoed around behind her for fear of bringing her back to reality. There were thick vines growing up the man's back and curling around his shoulders. Oranges and grapes, plumegranates and other less familiar fruit dangled from the vines. Tiny animals and glittering dragonflies sprang from the tip of the needle. It was certainly mesmerizing to watch, and when the tattoo was finally completed Bea had no idea how much time had passed.

"That will hurt for a few days and itch for a few more," said Ma as she soaped her hands in a basin. She fitted a new tip to the needle. "Wash with warm water, and don't take a bath till the itching stops. Next!"

Bea felt a light touch on her arm. It was Mrs. Miller, silent for once. She smiled and put her finger to her lips. Bea felt suddenly tired as she followed her up the ladder to the verandah. Phoebe was already there, perched on the edge of a chair and working her way through a bowl of thick stew. Willow was slumped in the other chair, staring ahead with dull eyes. As Bea sat down she remembered with a chill the words of the bald man at the Quorum as he listed the people who had been afflicted by the Ledbetter clan—*Little Erika Spivey. Jim Hooker. The Miller girl* . . . It was no wonder the Millers refused to mention the Ledbetters in front of their daughter.

She ate in silence the dinner that Mrs. Miller put before her, while Ma worked on tirelessly in the clearing below. The people in line showed no sign of giving up, waiting patiently for the opportunity to have themselves decorated with pictures of such surpassing beauty, and Mrs. Miller set up a circle of lamps around them as the light faded. Willow rose from her chair and drifted like a ghost into her room, and shortly afterward the verandah began to shake as Pa climbed the ladder. "Still up, eh, girls?" he said. He forced a smile onto his face, and Bea could see at once that he had heard nothing hopeful in his search. He disappeared into the kitchen and returned with a bottle of beer, which he uncapped with his teeth.

"Do you think Ma will work all night?" asked Bea.

Pa nodded. "There's a lot going on in her head right now," he said, "and it has to come out somehow." He took a long draft of beer and wiped the back of his mouth with a sigh. "It's been a long time," he said.

Bea sank back into the soft cushions of the cane chair. She thought about going to bed, but before she could summon the energy to get up she felt herself slipping away into sleep. The buzzing of the tattoo machine wound through her dreams like an echo of childhood, while above her in the corner bedroom Willow Miller sat propped up by pillows, twisting a corner of her nightgown between her fingers and waiting for the dawn.

# Sneaking

**B**ea Flint awoke to the sound of birds chattering in the trees. Someone had put a blanket over her in the night. She was stiff from sleeping curled up in the chair, and when she tried to open her eyes they felt gummy. She caught a glimpse of Mrs. Miller, sitting in a chair at the balcony's edge and stitching something. Bea closed her eyes again quickly. The sun was already high, but still it felt too early for talking. She pictured Theo waiting for her where the thin wavy trees were, and felt the weight of his absence at once like a cold stone in the pit of her stomach.

She tried to distract herself by listening to the bird-song that surrounded her. There was a colony of small birds in the Millers' own tree. She could hear the *chip-chip-cheeep* of a hundred small chicks, their beaks open to the sky as they yelled for their breakfast, and the chatter of their parents as they squabbled over who should provide it. There was another larger bird there too. He sang a longer song that ran out like a telephone wire toward a neighboring tree. He was answered by another, maybe a hundred paces away toward the falls. As her ears followed that sound, Bea became aware again of the network of bees that loosely tied the countryside together, and from the purposeful paths of the bees she learned that the line of villagers had gone and her mother was no longer in the clearing. She felt she was beginning to grasp the idea of Mumbo Jumbo, and she remembered what her grandmother had said: *You are the one who can find Theo.* She sat up at once and opened her eyes.

"I've made you both some sandwiches," said Mrs. Miller quietly. She smiled at her. "Of course, you can have breakfast here if you like, but I expect you'll want to set off exploring as soon as you can."

Bea rubbed her eyes with her knuckles. Mrs. Miller had resumed her sewing, and there was a pile of sandwiches on the table, neatly wrapped in waxed paper. "Have you been there all night?" asked Bea.

"I couldn't sleep," said Mrs. Miller, "and you both

looked so comfortable there I didn't want to wake you."

"Thank you," said Bea. She looked at Phoebe on the chair beside hers, tucked up in another blanket and still fast asleep. She poked her with her toe.

Phoebe sprang to life like a jack-in-the-box. "Let's go!" she said.

They set off along the path, warmed by two mugs of steaming hot chocolate that Mrs. Miller had insisted on making for them. They had told her that they would return to the hills where they had been the previous day, but once they were out of sight of the house they doubled back to visit Arkadi. Phoebe trailed a stick on the ground and said thoughtfully, "He can't be the one Granny Delphine was talking about. He'd have to be a hundred and forty at least."

"What age would you say he is?" asked Bea. She had made a small opening in the zipper of the backpack and was feeding almonds to Nails as they walked.

"It's hard to tell," said Phoebe. "Forty? Sixty? He can't be a *hundred* and forty. Nobody's that old."

"Maybe," said Bea, "but how many . . ." She paused. She had heard something odd to her right. There were so many sounds among the trees that she could not tell what it was. Some tiny sound, so faint that it was almost no sound at all. That was it! No sound at all. She resumed talking, but her ears tuned in like satellite dishes. She could almost feel them swiveling. "How many people do you know named Arkadi?"

"None," said Phoebe. "I don't know any other Phoebes either, but that doesn't mean I'm a hundred and forty."

Bea lowered her voice. "Don't look around," she said, "but Granny Delphine was right. Someone is following us."

"One of the Ledbetters?" whispered Phoebe.

"Must be."

"Is it the same one who was spying on us when we went back to the falls?"

"I don't know," said Bea. "I can't see him."

"You heard him, right?" said Phoebe. She was starting to get used to her friend's unusual hearing.

"Sort of. It's more that I can't hear him."

"Then how do you know he's there?"

"You know how sneaky the Ledbetters are," said Bea quietly. "They're so good at creeping up on people that they don't make a sound."

"Are you going to start making sense soon?" said Phoebe.

Bea laughed. "There are bees and crickets and shrews

and all sorts of creatures in the undergrowth," she explained. "They're moving around all the time, but when a Ledbetter passes they freeze until he's gone. It's like a patch of silence moving through the trees." She felt a wave of delight at her newfound skill. "It's a dead giveaway!" she whispered.

"We'll have to lose him," said Phoebe. "Otherwise we'll lead him straight to Arkadi."

"That won't be easy," said Bea.

"We'll split up."

"He'll still follow me," said Bea. "Maize will have told him to stick with me."

"Where is he now?" said Phoebe.

Bea tuned herself in to the silence. "About twenty feet to the right of the path, and ten paces behind us. What are you—"

"Meet you at the falls," whispered Phoebe. She stopped in her tracks. "Was that a sausageberry tree back there?" she said in a loud voice, and in an instant she was gone, charging straight through the trees toward the sneaking silence. Bea caught a glimpse of the spy as he tried to slip out of Phoebe's path. It was a Ledbetter, all right; there was no mistaking that broad blank face. It looked like the boy who had fallen into the thorn-bush at the Millers' house, the boy whom Maize had called Ike. Like all his clan he seemed to be wrapped for a blizzard.

Bea quickly stepped out of sight to the left of the path. She lost herself among the trees, keeping low for the protection of the ferns and bushes. When she judged she had gone far enough she stopped, crouched down, and listened. The sounds of the forest assembled themselves around her, but she could hear nothing out of place. She smiled. She could see the little hut among the trees, and she made her way toward it.

She moved as quietly as she could, trying to be as stealthy as their pursuer, but she soon learned just how difficult that was. The birds called her position cheerfully to one another. Small animals scurried through dried leaves to avoid her, and twigs snapped beneath her feet. *Just as they always do in stories*, she thought. *It must take a lifetime of sneaking around to be that good at it.*

Arkadi sat with his back to her. He was peeling some sort of yellow fruit and humming to himself. Bea held her breath and tiptoed even more carefully.

"I finished the doggie," said Arkadi. He put the fruit down carefully on a leaf and turned around. He produced the carving from his overalls pocket. "Do you like it?"

Bea let her breath out with a whoosh. "It's not a

doggie," she said, slightly irritated. "It's a meerkat." She looked closely at the carving. It was incredibly detailed. It stood with its nose in the air, and it was so lifelike that she could almost see it twitch. "It's very good!" she said.

Arkadi beamed. "I like making things," he said. "Did you bring sandwiches?"

Bea put the backpack on the ground and unzipped the front pocket. She found it impossible to remain annoyed with Arkadi. "I don't know what's in them," she said.

Arkadi unwrapped a sandwich and took an enormous bite. "Fwhere's your ffriend?" he said through stuffed cheeks.

"Someone was following us, so Phoebe went the other way to distract him."

Arkadi nodded. "Big eyes, all wrapped up," he said. "I've seen him."

"Do you think he saw you?" asked Bea.

Arkadi shook his head. "I'm good at hiding."

"Because of Mumbo Jumbo?" said Bea. She held her breath, waiting for his answer.

"Don't know about any of that stuff," said Arkadi, wiping his mouth on his sleeve. "I'm always getting in trouble. That's why I'm good at hiding."

"My granny says Mumbo Jumbo was founded by a man named Arkadi," said Bea.

"I heard that too," said Arkadi. "Are there any more sandwiches?"

Bea gave him another. She rushed her next question out before she could feel too foolish to ask it.

"Are you the same Arkadi?"

Arkadi did not laugh. His face remained as open as before.

"It was a popular name when I was little," he said. "Every Tom, Dick and Harry was called Arkadi."

Bea heard a sound behind her and turned quickly around. Phoebe was coming through the trees, scratched and smiling. "I lost him," she said.

Bea turned back, but Arkadi had vanished. The meerkat carving stood on the log where he had sat a moment before, an inquisitive little figure in blond wood. The hut yawned open, as though it had been empty for years. Bea looked over Phoebe's shoulder. She could see no movement among the trees, but she shook her head. "I don't think you did," she whispered.

# Books

"I didn't really get a proper answer," said Bea. "He just said that Arkadi was a popular name; then you turned up and he disappeared before I could ask him any more." They sat on the mossy rock near Cambio Falls. Here in the water's roar they could talk without fear of being overheard, while Nails sniffed around in the grass, stopping now and then to tug a worm from the soft earth.

"Sorry," said Phoebe. "Do you think he's gone like . . . like Theo?"

Bea shook her head. "He's just good at hiding. He must have known the Ledbetter spy was still behind you."

"How can we go looking for Theo with that Ledbetter creep following us?" said Phoebe. "If we did find Theo they would know straightaway."

Bea scuffed the grass with her toe. "I don't see the point in going back to the copses to look for him anyway. We're never going to find him just by wandering around aimlessly." She wanted more than anything to take out the Squeak Jar and speak to Theo, but she was afraid that the sight of the jar might provide some clue that their stalker could bring to Maize Ledbetter. They had eaten the remaining sandwiches sometime earlier, and waited around in the faint hope that the Ledbetter boy would get bored and leave. Bea pictured Maize Ledbetter's menacing stare, and she knew that it was not likely.

"Granny Delphine thinks you can find him," said Phoebe.

"She means by using Mumbo Jumbo, but I'm not even sure what that is. It might take years to learn."

"If Arkadi was the real Arkadi I bet he could help you," said Phoebe.

"If he was the real Arkadi he wouldn't admit to it. Otherwise why would he be hiding? Besides, we can't even go back and find him. Not as long as we have the creep on our tail."

"Is he still there?"

Bea nodded. Even in the roar of the falls she could still sense the odd patch of silence that betrayed the

Ledbetter boy's presence.

"Why do you think they wear all those scarves and gloves?" said Phoebe.

"I keep wondering that. Maybe they're always cold."

Phoebe was quiet for a minute; then she said, "There must be someone we could ask about Arkadi."

"I don't see how we can ask anyone without giving him away, and I don't really want to do that. What if he is just a harmless simpleton?"

"We could tell Bontoc. It was probably him who locked Arkadi into the Blue Moon Mobile in the first place."

"I haven't seen Bontoc since the night we arrived."

"We could try his office in the library. At least the Ledbetter spy won't be able to follow us in there without being seen."

"I don't know what time the library . . . ," began Bea; then a sudden thought struck her. "Of course! Bell Hoot Library. They're sure to have a book on Arkadi, since he founded the place." She jumped up and hastily packed the backpack. "We can look him up and see what he looked like."

They walked quickly back in the direction of the library. Bea tried to ignore the uncomfortable patch of silence that followed them at a short distance, but they spoke in whispers nonetheless. The library was cool inside. The floor was polished wood and the tall bookcases formed a bewildering maze. Just inside the door was a wooden desk, and on it a brass sign engraved with the word *Sssssssh!* The librarian was none other than Miss Hopkins, the typewriter lady from Captain Bontoc's office. She was rearranging cards in a dark green box.

"Hello," said Phoebe. Miss Hopkins looked up and gave them a gap-toothed smile. She put her finger to her lips and pointed at the brass sign.

"We're looking for a book about Arkadi," whispered Bea. "Do you have any?"

"Indeed we do," Miss Hopkins whispered back. There was no sign of anyone else in the library. "Do you have a library card?"

Bea frowned. "We just got here," she said.

"So you did," said Miss Hopkins. She handed them two narrow forms and a pencil each. There was only one question at the top of each form. It said simply:

*Well?*

Bea thought for a moment; then she wrote: *I would like to join the library. My name is Bea Flint, and I'm staying with the Millers at the moment.*

Phoebe licked her pencil, then wrote carefully on her own form: *We are looking for a book about Arkadi. My name is an anagram of* blue hope.

Miss Hopkins took the two forms and read them. She produced two green cards from a drawer and wrote the girls' names, one on each. She wrote *Phoebe Lu* without hesitation, and stamped the reverse of the cards in slow motion so as not to make a sound.

"Where will we find it?" whispered Bea.

"Find what?" said Miss Hopkins. She spoke so quietly that it was easier to lip-read than to hear her.

"The book about Arkadi," said Bea.

"It's on the top shelf at the back," said Miss Hopkins.

Bea looked at the shelf that Miss Hopkins indicated. It was the highest shelf of a very tall bookcase that stretched up to the floor of Captain Bontoc's suspended office. "Could you get it for us, please?" she said.

Miss Hopkins shook her head. "I'm afraid not," she said. "It's restricted. You'll need a note from the Quorum."

"But the Quorum only meets once a week," said Bea.

"Once a fortnight, dear," said Miss Hopkins. "But we've got plenty of other books to keep you amused in the meantime. We've got ones on abseiling, animals, archery, baking, bees, cakes, clothes, crossbows, dams, dreams, eating, eggs—"

"Yes, thank you," said Bea. "We'll take a look around."

They wandered in among the bookshelves until they were out of sight of the librarian.

"We're still whispering," muttered Phoebe, pulling a book from the nearest shelf. "I thought we came in here so we could talk."

"Never mind that," said Bea. "We have to get hold of that book."

"I could climb up there," said Phoebe. "But she'd see us."

Miss Hopkins billowed around the corner of a bookcase. "We'll be closing in ten minutes," she whispered. "I have to go upstairs to lock the filing cabinets. If you borrow any books just take the little cards out of the inside covers and drop them on my desk as you leave, like good girls." She flipped open a book and mimed the act of removing the card in case they were in any doubt; then she replaced it on the shelf. Bea saw her glance up at the top shelf where the restricted books were kept; then she turned and trotted up the creaking stairs to Captain Bontoc's office.

"I could probably get up there and back down before she comes out again," whispered Phoebe.

Bea shook her head. "She'd notice it was gone," she

said. She frowned for a moment in concentration. The sound of metal drawers being closed rolled from the office above like distant thunder. "I've got a better idea," said Bea. She took two books at random and quickly removed the little cards from inside. "Follow me," she whispered, and she ran quietly to the front desk. She could hear Miss Hopkins's key turn in the lock of the filing cabinet upstairs. "Quickly," she said. She dropped the two cards on the desk and pulled Phoebe after her as she ducked behind the nearest bookshelf.

The door of Captain Bontoc's office closed, and Miss Hopkins tripped lightly down the stairs. They listened to her bustling about quietly behind her desk for a while. She hummed to herself, a hum so faint that even Bea could barely detect it. Miss Hopkins allowed the tiniest jangle to escape from her keys as she removed them from her handbag and stepped out onto the porch. Just before she closed and locked the door, Bea caught sight of a boy sitting with his back against a tree on the far side of the clearing. It was unmistakably Ike Ledbetter, and his large pale eyes stared straight into hers for a moment before the library door closed softly and blocked him from view.

# Dust

**B**ea Flint and Phoebe Lu waited awhile to make sure that Miss Hopkins didn't return. The evening sunlight shone through the tall windows, casting yellow rectangles on the bookshelves. As the sun began to dip below the tree line the yellow rectangles rolled themselves up slowly like luminous blinds.

"Now what?" said Phoebe, still whispering from habit.

"Now you can climb up and get that book," said Bea. "It shouldn't take long to find out what we need to know; then we can put it back and get out through a window. Nobody will know we've looked at it."

They tiptoed back to the bookshelf at the back wall. "Wait a moment," said Bea. She peeped out of the nearest window into the twilit clearing. There was nobody in sight. The Ledbetter boy had finally left his post.

This did not come as the relief she had expected. At least when he was nearby she knew what he was up to. She wondered now what news he was bringing back to Maize Ledbetter, and she felt a sudden shiver. She turned around to see Phoebe perched at the top of the bookshelf.

"How do you spell *Arkadi*?" said Phoebe. Her voice echoed in the empty library.

"A-R-K—," began Bea.

"Found it!" said Phoebe. She slid a fat volume from the top shelf and dropped it without warning.

"Ouch!" said Bea, as the book dropped into her out-stretched hands like a leather-bound brick. "Careful!"

"Sorry," said Phoebe, who was back on the floor in an instant. "I had no free hands and it wouldn't fit in my mouth."

Bea blew the dust off the book's spine and placed it on the floor where a patch of dim light filtered in from the evening sky. There were lamps on the reading desks, but she did not want to risk turning one on. She began to flick through the book. She found to her dismay that there were over six hundred pages. She looked first for a photograph of Arkadi, but there did not seem to be any. There were several drawings of him, mostly done from memory by Pearlseeds who had been his pupils or friends. They showed him with a variety of hairstyles, sometimes with a beard or mustache, sometimes clean shaven. He looked different in each one, and Bea could not decide whether any of them looked like the ice-cream mechanic or not.

Phoebe showed little interest in the book. She prowled around the library looking for places to climb, and took a couple of turns sliding down the long banister from Captain Bontoc's office, until Bea told her irritably to stop.

"Did you find anything?" she asked from the bottom of the stairs.

Bea shook her head. She was squinting at a blurry charcoal drawing of Arkadi. Of all the ones she had seen this one most resembled the ice-cream mechanic. She read the caption with difficulty in the fading light. "'Arkadi as drawn by Maize Ledbetter the year before her banishment.'"

She began to read from the text. "'Various accounts have been given of the falling-out between Arkadi and his favorite, young Maize Ledbetter. It was rumored that she had honed her powers to such a fine point that she could predict almost any event with complete clarity, and some Pearlseeds believed that it was a combination of jealousy and fear that led Arkadi to banish her along with her young husband. It seems more likely, however, that it was the girl's well-known fits of rage and her disregard for the protocols of Mumbo Jumbo that led Arkadi to conclude she was a danger to the entire movement. The place he chose for his former protégée's exile was the secret refuge of Bell Hoot, which Arkadi himself had discovered by accident less than a year previously.'"

Bea rubbed her eyes. At that moment the moon emerged from behind a cloud and lit the open book with a pale blue glow. The smudgy image of Arkadi seemed to spring to life, and Bea was almost sure that it depicted the Arkadi they knew, despite the fact that it must have been drawn some eighty years earlier. She was about to turn the page in search of more information when a familiar phrase caught her eye: *the Hidden Boy*. Where had she heard that phrase recently? She read on. "'Many of the predictions made by Maize Ledbetter have since come true. Among those that she repeated most frequently was that she would live for a century, and that her successor as head of the Ledbetter clan would be a young child known only as the Hidden Boy.'"

Bea stopped reading. The skin crawled on the back of her neck. *Give us the Hidden Boy.* That was the demand of the Ledbetters when they invaded people's dreams. Granny Delphine believed that it referred to Theo, and Maize Ledbetter had made no effort to deny it. Bea looked around her. The bookcases loomed over her in the dark, and the library suddenly seemed an unwelcoming place. She closed the book. "Phoebe?" she said. Phoebe was at her elbow in a moment. "Let's put this back and get out of here," said Bea.

"You'll have to lend me the backpack to carry it up in," said Phoebe. "But I don't think we'll be leaving here until the morning."

Bea looked at her with a sinking feeling. "What do you mean?" she asked.

"I've tried all the windows," said Phoebe. "They're painted shut, every one of them. They mustn't have been opened for years."

"What about the door?"

Phoebe shook her head. "Locked with a key," she said. "I think we'd better make ourselves comfortable."

They did another complete circuit of the library, double-checking the windows in case they had missed one that could be opened. They searched the desk for a spare key to the front door, but without success. "Pa will come looking for us when we don't arrive home," said Bea.

"We'll be in trouble," said Phoebe.

Bea shivered. "I'd rather be in trouble than spend the night in here," she said. "Anyway, we can pretend we got locked in by accident."

They released Nails from the backpack and put in the book instead. Phoebe climbed the bookshelves and replaced it among the other books. They looked out into the clearing again, but it was deserted. Bea turned on a table lamp so that if anyone came looking for them they would see the library was not empty.

They dragged two large armchairs out into the middle of the room and settled down to wait. Phoebe had found a large jotter and a pencil behind Miss Hopkins's desk and she began to draw a world where volcanoes spewed chocolate and people turned into dragonflies. Beside the things she drew she wrote the anagrams that popped into her head—nailed frogs and darling foes for *dragonflies*, coal ovens and oval cones for *volcanoes*. Bea took out the Squeak Jar and listened for Theo's voice. It took a few minutes to locate him. He was whispering for once.

"I can't talk now," he said. "The Tree People are listening. They were pretty annoyed when I tried to start a fire."

"Are you okay?" whispered Bea. She saw Phoebe glance up at her.

"I'm fine. We'll talk later, okay?"

"Okay," said Bea. She could try to find him in her dreams. She put the Squeak Jar down and went looking for a book about bees, then seated herself in the comfortable armchair with the jar and the book in her lap. Nails returned from his explorations, disappointed at the lack of insect life and the total absence of worms, and climbed into the backpack of his own accord. Bea began to read about the complex life of bees, trying to distract herself from the creeping sense of foreboding in her bones.

Outside the library window the blue moon shone down on clearing and forest. It shone on the churning pool of Cambio Falls, and beyond it on the still waters of Mumpfish Lake, dark as midnight and cold as last week's soup. It shone on the rickety wooden causeway that ran from the bare island to the lakeshore. It shone on the blank-eyed, straggle-haired Ledbetter clan, who ran silently along the causeway and slipped into the shadows of the forest, drifting from tree to tree like blown ash, heading for the Bell Hoot Library.

# Dreaming

**B**ea Flint sat in the armchair and struggled to keep her eyes open. The book lay on her lap, words crawling over the pages like bees. She looked up at Phoebe, who had her head down and was drawing busily.

"We can talk now," said Theo's voice in her ear. "I promised them I wouldn't set fire to the trees again." Bea tried to look around, but she could not turn her head. She realized she must be dreaming.

"Where are you?" she asked.

"Right beside you. What's the book about?"

"Bees," said Bea.

Theo clucked scornfully. "Bees! That'd be like me reading a book about Theos. Is there such an animal as a Theo?"

"No. I'm only—," began Bea; then she stopped with

an effort. This was no time for silly arguments. "We went looking for you," she said.

"Oh, yeah," said Theo, "that reminds me: I figured out where I am."

Bea's eyes opened wide and she struggled to sit up. It felt as though an elephant sat on her chest. She frowned and tried to concentrate on Theo's words. "Tell me!" she said.

"Well," said Theo casually, "you know the way I said the trees were thin and wavy?"

Theo's voice itself seemed to be going thin and wavy, and Bea struggled to grasp what he was saying. Phoebe had abandoned her drawing and seemed to be squatting on the floor, staring hard at her. Her eyes had grown bigger and her armchair had evaporated. The library walls were moving closer, and there were fewer bookshelves. No, Bea corrected herself, there were no bookshelves at all.

Panic rose in her chest. She looked closely at the figure in front of her. Something was wrong. "You're not Phoebe!" she said. How could she have mistaken this blank-faced person for her friend? It wasn't even a girl. It was . . . She couldn't remember the name. He squatted before her. With an enormous effort Bea managed to turn her head and look around her. There was no sign of anyone else. "Theo?" she said. Her voice was deadened by the damp white walls, and there was no answer. She turned back to face the stranger, her eyes pricking with tears. "What have you done with Theo?" she choked.

The pale eyes stared at her, neither friendly nor hostile. She remembered who it was now. Ike Ledbetter, the boy who had been following them, the boy who had fallen into the thornbush. He had looked slightly helpless then, but he did not look helpless now. He looked right at home, squatting there before her. He had been in her dream only minutes—or was it hours?—but already she could tell that he would never leave.

Ike Ledbetter opened his colorless lips. "Give us the Hidden Boy," he said.

Bea felt a hand on her shoulder, shaking her awake. She was back in the library, dimly lit by a table lamp. She struggled from her chair, desperate to escape the traces of her dream. She felt a weight slide from her lap and heard the dull thump of the book and the clunk of the heavy jar hitting the wooden floor at the same time. She gasped with fright, but the Squeak Jar rolled away unbroken and came to rest beneath a bookshelf.

"Are you all right, child?" said Granny Delphine's voice. Bea barely heard her. She scrambled after the jar, feeling Ike Ledbetter's stare clinging to her skin like a damp cobweb. She reached for the Squeak Jar in the shadow of the bookcase. It was reassuringly whole. Her fingers brushed against something round and flat on the floor beside it. It took her a moment to realize what it was. The lid! It must have come off with the impact. Bea's heart sank.

She grabbed the lid and fumbled it back into place, screwing it tight. For how many seconds had the jar been open? Would a voice escape like a puff of air, or linger in the jar like smoke? She remembered Captain Bontoc's urgent shout when Ma had tried to unscrew the lid at Cambio Falls, and she felt a tightness in her chest as she picked up the Squeak Jar and rose unsteadily to her feet. What if Theo were gone for good?

Granny Delphine took the jar gently from Bea's hands and placed it on a table. She held Bea's shoulders and looked into her face. "Are you all right?" she asked again.

Bea nodded numbly. She could see Pa over Granny Delphine's shoulder, shoving the armchairs back against the wall, and Miss Hopkins hovering nervously with a set of keys dangling from one plump finger.

She did not want to tell her grandmother about Ike. It had been her foolish idea to hide in the library without checking that escape would be possible. She did not know how she would make things right, but she was sure it was something that she alone would have to do. With a huge effort she smiled and looked straight into her grandmother's eyes. "I'm fine," she said. "We got locked in by mistake, that's all."

"Just as well you were locked in," said Pa, dusting his hands. "That weird bunch were staring in the windows when we got here, all wrapped up like deranged carol singers. Don't know what they'd be wanting to steal from a library. Can't exactly see them running a book club."

"The Ledbetters were here?" said Phoebe, and Bea knew at once from her wide-eyed look that no Ledbetter had managed to invade her dreams.

"They looked like they were trying the windows," said Pa, who obviously had no idea what the Ledbetters were really up to, "but we soon sent them packing. Then your granny went off to get Miss Hopkins here to open the place up."

"Which would not have been necessary," said Granny

Delphine frostily, "if Miss Hopkins would think to check her library for stragglers before locking up for the night."

"It wasn't her fault," said Bea quickly. "We—"

"We went back at the last minute to look for another book," said Phoebe.

"And we didn't hear the door closing," finished Bea. She closed her tired eyes for a moment, but Ike Ledbetter's stare appeared in the darkness, and she opened them straightaway.

"Come," said Granny Delphine. Bea picked up the Squeak Jar and slipped it into the backpack beside the sleeping meerkat. Her bones felt like lead and she wanted nothing more than to be picked up by Pa and carried home, but she was determined to hide at least one thing from her grandmother's sharp eyes. If the Squeak Jar really was empty and her dreams were squatted by the Ledbetters, she no longer had any way to speak to Theo, and she was afraid that Granny Delphine would lose confidence in her. She made up her mind that she would have to confront Arkadi first thing in the morning. She was as sure as she could be that he was the real Arkadi, and she would threaten to expose him unless he could help her find her brother.

She was so wrapped up in her thoughts that they were halfway home before she realized they had left the library. Pa and Phoebe were some way ahead, and Granny Delphine seemed to be walking deliberately slowly so as to be able to speak without being overheard.

"I suppose you knew we were in the library," said Bea.

"Of course," said Granny Delphine. "You were reading more about Arkadi. That showed initiative, although you should know that Mumbo Jumbo cannot be learned from a book."

"How did you know—," began Bea.

"That you were reading up on Arkadi?" said Granny Delphine. "Why don't you tell me?"

Bea tried to imagine herself in Granny Delphine's place, sitting on the verandah of the Millers' house as the evening light faded. She knew that Granny Delphine used her eyes more than her ears in practicing Mumbo Jumbo, and she tried to visualize what her grandmother would have seen. "You saw it was getting dark and we weren't back yet," she began.

"Skip the obvious, child," said her grandmother curtly.

"You didn't see the Ledbetters," said Bea. "They

would have come from the direction of the lake." She hesitated. "I'm not sure how you knew we were in the library."

"I didn't," said Granny Delphine.

Bea frowned. "Then you were heading for Cambio Falls to look for us," she said. "You knew a Ledbetter would be spying on us, and that we could talk there without being heard."

"Correct," said her grandmother.

"Then you saw the Ledbetters at the library window and the light on inside, and you guessed we were in there. You knew Miss Hopkins wouldn't have locked us in by mistake, so we must have tricked her, which meant we were looking for something we weren't supposed to have." She thought for a moment, but she had reached a blank. "There's a whole shelf of restricted books. How did you know we wanted a book on Arkadi?"

"What did you do when you took down the book?" said Granny Delphine. "Think, Bea."

"I put it on the floor to read it."

"Before that?"

"I . . . I blew the dust off it," said Bea. "You looked on the restricted shelf and saw that it was cleaner than the others."

"Well done."

"But it was dark in the library," said Bea. "There was only a lamp on the table."

"I've got very good spectacles," said her grandmother.

Bea glanced at her. She wondered whether to mention the fact that she had tried out her grandmother's spectacles before they left for their holiday, then thought better of it. "Do they help you to . . . to see more?" she asked.

Granny Delphine threw her a sharp look. "Of course, child. That's what spectacles are for, isn't it?"

Bea changed the subject hastily. "How is all this going to help me find Theo?" she asked. She would have hesitated to ask Granny Delphine such a direct question only a few days before, but she no longer feared her grandmother's tongue. She was afraid now that Theo was slipping from her grasp, and getting to him as quickly as possible was the only thing that mattered.

"I can only give you the groundwork, Bea," said Granny Delphine. "I've been hiding for much of my life, and my powers are not well developed." She sighed. "Your ma has far more natural aptitude for it than I will ever have."

"*Ma* has?" said Bea, surprised.

"Certainly. I could see it from the moment she was born, but the Gummint was cracking down hard even then, and in school they taught her to fear even the mention of Mumbo Jumbo. She never became what she could have been. There are Pearlseeds here who are far more advanced in Mumbo Jumbo than either of us."

"Couldn't they find Theo?"

Granny Delphine shook her head. "You have a close connection to your brother. That is why you can hear his voice when even Captain Bontoc could not. It will take the combined efforts of the Quorum to teach you what you need to know, but you must find him yourself."

"But I don't have time for lessons," said Bea. "You can tell so many things just by looking and listening. Isn't that what I need to learn?"

"Learning to read the world is only the foundation of Mumbo Jumbo," said Granny Delphine. "It's like learning what all the lights and levers in a cockpit are for. That's all very interesting, but then you must learn to fly the airplane."

Bea thought about this for a moment. "Is that why things seem to do what Mrs. Miller wants them to, without her having to touch them?"

"Precisely," said Granny Delphine. "There's more to Gladys Miller than serving food and talking incessantly. She is a very powerful Pearlseed, but looking after Willow saps all her energy at the moment." She lowered her voice as they approached the bottom of the ladder. "Every Pearlseed has their specialty. Hers lies in manipulating objects with her thoughts. Maize Ledbetter can manipulate thoughts themselves, if she is close enough to see her victim."

Bea shuddered. That would explain why the Ledbetters liked to peer in through windows at night.

"I have pointed out to the Quorum that the Ledbetter problem is tied up with Theo's disappearance, since it appears to be him they are after. I have been trying to persuade them that they must pool their skills to help you in your search."

"Isn't there someone who knows all the skills?" whispered Bea as she climbed the ladder behind her grandmother.

Granny Delphine stopped at the top of the ladder and looked down at her. "Only Arkadi knew them all," she said.

Bea climbed the last few rungs, her heart thumping.

She felt that she would faint from the weight of Ike Ledbetter's stare. She threw herself down in a chair. She could hear Granny Delphine and Mrs. Miller talking in the kitchen, and she realized she hadn't eaten for hours.

Clockwork Gabby emerged ticking onto the verandah. She seemed to have acquired some of Mrs. Miller's whirlwind qualities, and within seconds the low table was piled with an assortment of foods. Phoebe filled her plate and attacked her supper with gusto. Bea sat up with effort and picked up a plumegranate. It felt cold and waxy. She put it to her lips, but could not bring herself to take a bite. She noticed Willow staring at her from the chair opposite. She smiled weakly and put down the untouched fruit.

Phoebe stretched and jumped up from her seat. "I'm going to bed," she said, and she crawled through the window behind her chair because it was more interesting than using the door.

Bea lay slumped in the wicker chair, staring at the lamp that hung in the far corner. Around the house the crickets kept up a constant chirruping, like a thousand tiny sewing machines working at full tilt. The lamps burned on, their wicks hissing quietly, and in the distance the bees wound down their operations for the night. Bea felt unable to move.

Presently Gabby came back to clear up the dishes. She looked at Bea and shook her head sadly. "Dream-shut," she said, and she ticked back into the house under a tower of plates.

Bea saw Willow get up from her chair and walk over to her. She felt the girl's limp hand on her shoulder. "She *knows*," said Willow. Her dark eyes looked searchingly into Bea's for a moment; then she turned and disappeared into the house without another word.

# Silence

**B**ea Flint sat in her bed and stared at the wardrobe on the far wall. In the dim light of dawn the knotty wood made itself into pictures—a silhouette of a little man writing with a huge quill, and above it a face with a twisted mouth, which changed into a strange knobbly landscape when she looked at it for long enough. She had been staring at these patterns for hours and already she hated them. Several times her eyes had closed without her permission, and she had had to pinch herself to stay awake.

She reached into Theo's backpack and took out the Squeak Jar. She placed it on her lap and looked at it for a while. She knew now how her mother had felt when she first listened for Theo's voice at Cambio Falls. She wanted to put off for as long as possible the terrible moment when she might put her ear to the jar and hear nothing. The face in the wardrobe door leered at her, daring her to listen. She put the horn to her ear with a sinking feeling. "Theo?" she whispered. There was only silence. The jar felt cold and empty in her hand, and she knew with a terrible certainty that Theo's voice had left it for good. She wiped her eyes with the back of her hand, and replaced the jar carefully in the backpack.

Eventually her head nodded and she slipped straight into a dream. She was trapped in a blank room again, with Ike Ledbetter squatting before her. His stare was mildly accusing, as though she might have slapped him in the face on some occasion she could not quite remember. She tried to speak, but her mouth was bone-dry and her tongue would not move.

Eventually Ike spoke. "Give us the Hidden Boy," he said.

Bea jerked awake. Her skin felt clammy. The light was the same as before, and in the other bed Phoebe slept peacefully, her breathing slow and shallow. Bea dressed quietly and crept down the stairs. She let herself out onto the verandah. The ladder crouched at the verandah's edge like a sleeping insect. She could almost see the life in the ladder as it waited to open itself. She concentrated hard. "Ladder," she said quietly. She was sure it was on the verge of unfolding. It was just waiting for her to really believe she could do it. "Ladder," she said again.

There was an echo to her voice this time, and to her astonishment the ladder tipped itself smartly over the edge of the verandah and met the ground with a *clack-clack-thump*. Bea could not believe her eyes. She would have been impressed if she had even made it twitch. She had a sudden feeling she was being watched, and looked around quickly at the house.

Willow Miller was leaning out of her bedroom window. "Go on, then," she said flatly.

Bea felt herself deflate as she realized where the echo had come from. "That was you," she said.

"Of course," said Willow. "Hurry up if you're going. It's cold hanging out of this window."

Bea climbed swiftly down the ladder and stepped onto the dew-soaked grass.

"Ladder," said Willow from the window, and the ladder creaked reluctantly back into place.

"Thanks, Willow," said Bea.

Willow shrugged. "Good luck," she said, and she closed the window.

Bea turned and ran lightly along the path in the

direction of the falls. She dreaded passing beneath the blank gaze of the library's windows, but she did not want to risk getting lost looking for an alternative route. She kept her eyes down and ran on, light-headed from lack of sleep. She plunged into the woods when she judged she was near Arkadi's hut. Brambles scratched her legs, but she barely noticed. She could not detect Ike's presence anywhere nearby. *He probably doesn't have to follow me anymore*, she thought, and she wondered with a shiver if he could see any of her thoughts when she dreamed of him.

When she reached the hut she found the door standing open, and the hut looked empty. Her heart sank. "This is no time to be hiding," she said aloud.

"I'm not hiding," said Arkadi. "I'm washing." He was stripped to the waist and half hidden by a broad tree trunk. In front of him was a battered basin filled with water.

"I need your help," said Bea. She glanced at Arkadi's skinny body and was about to look away when she noticed that he had a tattoo on his left shoulder blade. Arkadi met her eye and pulled on his grubby T-shirt, but not before she had seen what the tattoo depicted. It was old and the lines had softened with the years, but she could clearly see it was a meerkat, standing tall in a tuft of faded grass and looking out into the distance.

"You want something fixed?" said Arkadi.

"I want to find my brother," said Bea. "I need to learn Mumbo Jumbo."

"Just like that?" said Arkadi.

"I don't have any time left," said Bea. "I'm the only one who can find him."

"I don't know anything about Mumbo Jumbo," said Arkadi.

"You didn't know what a meerkat was either," said Bea, "but there's one tattooed on your shoulder. What did you ask the tattoo artist to draw—a doggie?"

Arkadi smiled. "You have a quick eye," he said. "And a sharp tongue. You get both from your grandmother."

Bea's heart quickened. "You know Granny Delphine?"

"Used to," said Arkadi, "a long time ago."

"Then you *are* the real Arkadi," said Bea. "Why are you hiding?"

"I have my reasons," said Arkadi.

"But nobody here has seen you for years. Wouldn't they be happy to know you're alive?"

"Some would, no doubt."

"Were you hiding all that time?"

Arkadi suddenly looked tired. "I was unavoidably detained," he said.

"But you're here now," persisted Bea. "Why don't you just—"

Arkadi interrupted her. "A river must flow from the mountain to the sea, but it never does so in a straight line. Why?"

Bea thought for a moment. "Because there are obstacles to go around."

"Perhaps," said Arkadi. "Did you bring sandwiches?"

"No," said Bea. "I got up before anyone. I couldn't sleep. Are you going to help me or not?"

"Not," said Arkadi.

"Then I'll have to report you to the Quorum," said Bea. "They need your help with the Ledbetters anyway. What good is hiding in the woods?"

"You made a promise."

"My little brother is missing. If I have to break a promise to find him then I will."

Arkadi gazed at her steadily for a while. After three days in hiding his hair was no longer slicked neatly back. It stuck out in all directions, reminding her of one of Theo's drawings with a scribble-fringed face. His eyes were calm, like the center of a storm. "Very well," he said. "Where do we start?"

Bea sat down on the log where Arkadi had whittled the meerkat the previous day. She had come out without the backpack, without Nails. She had not eaten, but neither did she have any appetite, and she felt giddy from lack of sleep. "Theo disappeared on the crossing," she said. "I was able to hear his voice from the Squeak Jar, but then I dropped it and the lid came off, and now I can't hear him anymore."

Arkadi winced. "That's not good," he said. "Did you get a chance to ask him where he was?"

"He said he was somewhere where the trees were thin and wavy. He's with some people he calls the Tree People. He was about to tell me where it was, but . . ."

"But you dropped the Squeak Jar?"

Bea shook her head. "I was able to hear him when I was dreaming too, but my dream was interrupted."

"Then you can ask him next time you're asleep."

"I can't sleep anymore," said Bea. Tears were starting at the corners of her eyes, and she blinked them back impatiently.

Arkadi clicked his tongue. "Ledbetter trouble, eh?" he said, as though he were talking of nothing more serious than a mosquito bite.

"How did you know?"

"Sounds like one of Maize's tricks," said Arkadi. "She was always knocking on people's skulls, that child, though it used to be just a game."

"She's hardly a child," said Bea. "She's almost a hundred."

Arkadi shook his head in puzzlement. For a moment he looked like the confused ice-cream mechanic again. "That long," he muttered.

"It's Ike Ledbetter who's squatting in my dreams," said Bea. "I think he's her grandson. Or maybe her great-grandson."

"Why don't you ask him to leave?"

Bea looked at Arkadi to see if he was joking. "I wish I could," she said.

"A wish is no good unless you can give it legs," said Arkadi.

"That's what Theo said," said Bea in surprise. "What does it mean?"

"It means that you can just wish something would happen, or you can try to figure out how to make it happen. Both are wishes, but the one with legs is more likely to get where it's going."

"It's not as simple as just asking him to leave," said Bea. "There are people all over Bell Hoot with . . . with Ledbetter trouble. One girl died yesterday. I *can't* make him leave. It's like he's glued to the floor."

"Glued, eh?" said Arkadi thoughtfully. "Tell me, whose dream is it?"

"It's mine," said Bea. "At least, I think so."

"Then everything in it is created by you," said Arkadi.

"Not Ike Ledbetter," said Bea.

"The Ike in your dream is," said Arkadi, "and so is the glue."

"That was just a phrase," said Bea. "The glue isn't real."

"It's as real as your dream. What do you suppose the glue is made of?"

Bea thought about this. She made herself picture her dream, and the immobile, blank-faced figure of Ike Ledbetter squatting before her. Arkadi was right: It was her dream, so what was it that made Ike impossible to remove? She remembered the feeling of her tongue sticking to her mouth, and her heart racing with fear. "Fear?" she said.

"That's a good answer," said Arkadi.

"Is it the right answer?"

"Maybe."

Bea felt a surge of irritation. It didn't sound like Arkadi was taking her situation seriously. "I thought you were supposed to be the master of Mumbo Jumbo," she said.

"So they say," said Arkadi mildly.

"Then why can't you tell me if it's the right answer?"

"Mumbo Jumbo isn't about answers," said Arkadi. "It's about asking the right questions. Like this one: How can you overcome your fear of Ike Ledbetter?"

Bea thought about the creeping Ledbetter clan. The very sight of them filled her with dread, ever since she had first seen them surrounding the Millers' house. She pictured them climbing silently toward the windows, and saw Ike tumble from the shoulders of the stocky man below him, and the momentary start of shock on his face as he fell into the thornbush. It was the only glimpse of weakness she had seen any Ledbetter show.

"I'll have to find out what he's afraid of?" she said.

"That's the right question," said Arkadi approvingly. He was silent for a while as he chewed on the end of a twig to make himself an impromptu toothbrush. "How is your mother holding up?" he asked presently.

"She took up tattooing again," said Bea. "That's what she used to do before Theo was born. She worked nonstop for two days until she'd tattooed everyone in sight. I think she was trying to distract herself."

"No doubt," said Arkadi. "Is that the only reason she did it?"

"What other reason would there be?"

"That's also the right question," said Arkadi. "What are the tattoos like?"

"I only saw one up close," said Bea. "It was beautiful. There was a lot of forest, and things hidden in it."

Arkadi raised his bushy eyebrows, but said nothing.

"Things hidden in the forest!" said Bea. It seemed so obvious now. "Granny Delphine said that Ma has a natural aptitude for Mumbo Jumbo, but that she was afraid to learn about it."

"Natural aptitudes have a way of coming out," said Arkadi. "I think a closer look at your mother's tattoos might be very instructive, don't you?"

Bea nodded. "Can I ask you something?" she said.

"Of course."

"Why did you pretend to be . . ." She searched for the right words.

"Not very bright?" suggested Arkadi.

"Yes."

"I needed you to trust me," said Arkadi. "It's easier to trust someone if you don't think they're capable of deception."

"I suppose."

"Do you trust me now?"

Bea looked at Arkadi. His face seemed as open as ever. "I think so," she said.

"Then let me give you one little piece of advice." He leaned closer to her and dropped his voice. "Those Tree People that your brother talks about—it might be best not to mention them to anyone else."

"Why?" said Bea. "Who are they?"

Arkadi straightened up. "No idea," he said cheerfully. "Have you?"

"No," said Bea.

"Then until we have a good reason to believe otherwise, we should leave them in peace, don't you think?"

"They might have kidnapped Theo," said Bea.

"Or they might have saved him," said Arkadi.

# Key

Bea Flint walked slowly back toward the Millers' house as the sun warmed the air and the bees went into busy mode. She came to the main square, where stallholders were setting up their weekly market around the broad steps of the library. There was bustle everywhere, and already the stalls were piled with colorful fruit, tools and plant pots, pickles and preserves, shoes, candles, colored glass, cloth by the yard, belts, buckles and bridles, songbirds in wicker cages, knives, ropes, maps, balms and bandages, pâtés and sausages, bread, books, and a hundred other things. She passed them by with barely a glance.

A pale fish stared sightlessly from a bed of ice on the last stall. Its colorless fat lips were frozen around its last gasp, giving it a witless expression that reminded her uncomfortably of Ike Ledbetter. She groaned. Even when she was awake she could not get Ike out of her mind. She knew what she had to do, but the prospect filled her with dread. She was so tired that it would be difficult not to fall asleep, but how was she to overcome her fear of the dream squatter? He had never even spoken to her, except to intone the demand of his clan: *Give us the Hidden Boy.*

It did not come as a surprise to her to find that the Millers' house was once again surrounded by people. At first she thought that news of Ma's tattooing skills had spread even further, but on second glance she noticed that the people bunched up around Ma in the clearing were already tattooed. They did not all seem entirely pleased about it either.

"I'm telling you it wasn't there yesterday," said a man with grizzly hair. He had his shirt rolled up to his armpits and was pointing to a figure half-hidden in the picture on his stomach. "When you done this it was all plants and birds. That was what I asked for. It ain't natural for new details to sneak out of a tattoo in the night."

"Same thing happened to mine," said a woman with elaborately decorated shoulders. "I've got bees everywhere now, where yesterday there was just flowers."

"You must be mistaken," Ma said to them.

"You can rest assured," said Pa, "that nobody will be charged for any extra details that may have emerged." He had descended the ladder to see what the commotion was about, and was now looming over the crowd. Looming was one of Pa's specialties.

"That's not the point," said the woman with the bees, a little doubtfully. "How do we know what might come out in the future?"

"Nothing will come out that isn't there already," said Pa. "My wife is the fastest tattooist in history. You just didn't notice all the details when they were being done."

Bea could see that Ma herself was a little shaken by the notion that her tattoos might be continuing to grow without her. The rings under her eyes were even darker than before, and she looked ten years older than she had when they set out for the holiday of a lifetime.

Bea stepped forward and cleared her throat. "Why don't we take a look at these tattoos," she said loudly. "Maybe we can figure out what's happening."

The townspeople looked around to see who was speaking. Ma and Pa looked at her too, surprise on their faces. There was no sign of Granny Delphine, but Bea could almost hear her grandmother's voice in her mind, and she knew just what she would say.

"Don't stand there gawping," she heard herself say. "Bring that bench over here and sit down in a line. We'll get to everyone, if you all have a bit of patience."

Grizzly Hair and another man went obediently to fetch the garden bench, and the tattooed and discontented sat themselves down in a line. They had stopped muttering now.

Bea put her arm around her mother's waist and gave her a quick squeeze. "Come on," she said. "Let's see what we can see."

Ma nodded. She looked at Bea as though she were seeing her for the first time.

"Where's Granny Delphine?" asked Bea.

"She's gone to the Quorum. She called another extraordinary meeting." Ma smiled weakly. "She's only just gotten here and already she's running the place."

Grizzly Hair was first on the bench. He was a pig farmer from just outside Bell Hoot, and since he made it a point always to test his own products for quality he had made a broad canvas of his belly over the years. Ma's artwork curled across it, a tangle of vines and mossy branches, dotted with brightly colored birds. He pointed at the offending figure. "This wasn't here before. I watched the whole thing being done, and I'd have seen it."

Bea peered closer. The figure of a girl was barely visible in the shadows. Her face was turned away, and she carried what appeared to be a large key. "Looks a bit like you, Bea," said Pa, leaning over Ma's shoulder.

"I don't remember putting you in," whispered Ma.

"You worked nonstop for two days," said Bea. "You couldn't remember every detail."

"Why's she holding a key?" said Pa.

Bea glanced at Ma. She remembered what Granny Delphine had said about Ma's aptitude for Mumbo Jumbo, and how Arkadi said that aptitudes had a way of coming out. She said nothing. Grizzly Hair looked at Ma expectantly, and Pa's question hung in the air. Suddenly Ma seemed to snap out of her daze. She took a deep breath, and some of the spark came back into her eyes. "Yes, of course I put her there," she said to the pig farmer. "I often put my children into my tattoos."

"But—"

Ma straightened up and gave Grizzly Hair a brilliant

smile. "You must have nodded off while I was putting her in."

"I'm sure I only asked for birds," muttered Grizzly Hair.

Pa loomed closer. "Are you saying you'd have preferred another parakeet to a picture of my daughter?"

"I . . . er . . . of course not," said the pig farmer hastily. He rolled his shirt down and got up from the bench. "Like you say, it was a long day. I must have been dozing. I was just curious."

"Thank you. Come again," Pa called after him as he hurried away.

"Next," said Bea. She was conscious of Ma looking at her as the tattooed townsfolk slid up along the bench.

"You've grown up all of a sudden," said Ma quietly.

Bea looked at her and smiled.

"Your grandmother says . . ." Ma hesitated. She seemed to change her mind. "You're carrying a key in that man's tattoo," she said.

"I know," said Bea. "Let's see what the next one shows."

The woman whose shoulders were tattooed with flowers was next in line. Among the flowers the bees were visible, making a complex pattern that Bea recognized from listening to the flight of the bees around her. She was pretty sure she could even tell which hive they came from. It wasn't long before the tattooed woman was convinced that the bees were a welcome addition to the flowers that curled around her shoulders. "The inks brighten up as the tattoo heals," said Ma brusquely. "That's when you can see things you hadn't noticed before."

"And what good are flowers without bees?" added Bea.

There were several more people waiting to have their tattoos inspected. They had arrived disgruntled, but having listened to Bea and her parents dealing with the first few complaints they were starting to see their evolving tattoos as a valuable novelty. They forgot their dissatisfaction, and lined up to have their tattoos admired and interpreted. Bea examined each picture carefully, noting especially the details that their owners said were new. She tried to make sure she remembered everything. The line eventually dwindled to nothing, and Bea climbed the ladder, followed by Ma and Pa, and sank onto one of the familiar cane chairs.

For a while she lay slumped in the chair, listening

to the reassuring pattern of the bees as they went about their business. She knew that bees had some part to play in solving this whole puzzle, but she could not yet imagine what it was. The details in Ma's tattoos buzzed around in her mind in no particular order: a stand of tall thin trees that might be the place where Theo was hidden, the girl with the key who looked like Bea herself, a bare island in still waters. Another tattoo featured mysterious figures wrapped in scarves and mittens that reminded Bea of the curiously over-dressed Ledbetters. Why would they choose to make their home in such a barren place? She was sure that if she could just line up all the tattoos in the right order the answer would be as clear as the water that cascaded over Cambio Falls.

Ma's voice broke through her thoughts. "Your grand-mother says that you're the only one who can find our Theo," she said.

Bea sat up with an effort. "She told me that too," she said.

"Do you think you can?"

"I hope so," said Bea, "but I have to sleep first."

"Sleep?" said Ma, shaking her head in puzzlement. "You can't sleep now, Bea. There's no time to waste."

Bea got to her feet. Her mother sat on the edge of her chair, worry stretching the skin on her face. Bea kissed her softly on the forehead. "Trust me, Ma. I have to sleep. It's the only way I can find him now."

"I don't understand," said Ma.

"I know," said Bea.

# Boat

B ea climbed the stairs slowly and closed the bedroom door behind her. Phoebe's bed was empty, but Bea was too tired to wonder where she had gone. She lay down and stared at the ceiling, trying to prepare for her encounter with Ike. She was not aware that she had fallen asleep until she found herself sitting in a plain room with her back to the wall. There he was, squatting against the wall opposite, his blank stare fixing her to the spot. He did not look as though he had blinked since she saw him last.

*Now,* she thought, *I have to ask him to leave.* She opened her mouth to speak, but her voice was stuck in her throat. Ike stared on. *He knows that I'm scared of him,* she thought helplessly. *How can I hide that from someone who's inside my head?*

She wondered if it would help to look away, but she could no more move her head than make her voice work. It seemed that the glue of fear that Arkadi had talked about bound her just as much as Ike. She had no choice but to stare back at him. His eyes were colorless and his face too smooth, as though he had not been finished properly. His mouth opened, reminding her of the fish in the market stall. "Give us the Hidden Boy," he said.

She caught that look again, as though she had somehow offended him, even though it was he who was intruding on her sleep and not the other way around. She remembered the first time she had seen him, pulling himself from the thornbushes and trotting after Maize Ledbetter like a whipped dog. Maize had called him an idiot boy, and he had thrown Bea and Phoebe a wounded look then too, as though they were responsible for getting him into trouble. A sudden thought flashed into her head. *That* was what he was afraid of. She opened her mouth and forced the name out through lips as dry as cuttlebone. "Maize," she croaked.

At the mention of the old woman's name, Ike gave a tiny start. It was a mere flicker of uncertainty, but it was enough.

She tried again. "Maize sent you." She could see

worry creeping into his eyes. The glue seemed to melt a little.

Ike opened his mouth as though to answer, then changed his mind. "Give us the Hidden Boy," he said instead.

"Is that all you can say?" said Bea.

Ike shifted uncomfortably.

"You don't have to sit there staring at me just because Maize tells you to," said Bea. "Why don't you leave me alone?"

"You got to give us the Hidden Boy first," said Ike.

A giddy feeling came over Bea, as though her stomach had turned into a helium balloon. It was a tiny variation on the Ledbetters' usual words, but it was a reply rather than a demand. The giddy feeling passed just as quickly, leaving her with a chill. "A girl died the other day from . . . from not sleeping or eating," she said. "Did you know that?"

Ike shrugged. "Everyone dies," he said.

"Not that way," said Bea angrily.

"You got to give us the Hidden Boy," Ike repeated.

"If you mean Theo, I couldn't even if I wanted to. I don't know where he is. Nobody does."

Ike settled back into his squatting position. His

instructions were to stay until they got the Hidden Boy. That was simple enough.

A thought struck Bea. "What are you really doing?" she asked. "I mean, while you're in my dream. Do you have to be asleep too?"

Ike looked puzzled. He was not used to such questions. He thought for a moment. "No," he said finally. "First time I got to get a look at you to find the way in, but after that I just got to stop what I'm doing. I got to think hard."

"What were you doing just now?" asked Bea.

"Making a boat."

"Really?" Bea was genuinely surprised. "I wouldn't have a clue how to do that."

"It's easy," said Ike. "Well, sort of." A spark glowed briefly in his eyes. It looked like the boat was something that he kept very much to himself.

"I bet it isn't," said Bea.

"It's my third boat," said Ike. "You learn more each time."

"Why don't you go back to work on it now. Then I can get some rest, and you can be doing what you like."

Ike shook his head. "I got to stay here," he said.

"Nobody will know," Bea persisted. "I'm hardly

going to tell Maize, am I? Anyway, she thinks you're stupid. I heard her call you 'idiot boy.'"

Ike looked at his feet. "I'm not stupid," he said sullenly.

"Maybe you are," said Bea, "and maybe you're not. How smart is it to be sitting here staring at me when you could be working on your boat?"

The boy stared at her with his pale eyes. He was confused now. He couldn't remember having had a conversation like this before, either dreaming or waking. Things had been very simple until this girl started asking awkward questions. Now he didn't know what to do. "You won't tell?" he said at last.

"Of course not," said Bea. Ike looked at her a moment longer; then he melted into the wall behind him and was gone.

Bea stared at the empty spot for a moment, not daring to believe her eyes. She had gotten rid of him, and it hadn't been as hard as she had imagined. Now that she was free of Ike she could try to find Theo again. She was still in the blank room, but she supposed it was as good a place as any to start from. "Theo?" she said aloud.

"It's me, Phoebe," said Phoebe's voice urgently.

Bea frowned. That wasn't right. Someone was shaking her shoulder.

"Wake up," said Phoebe.

Bea opened her eyes and found herself back in her bedroom in the Millers' house. "What did you wake me for?" she said, the sleep slowly draining from her. "I was just about to speak to Theo."

"Granny Delphine wants you," said Phoebe. "You've been summoned by the Quorum. They want to hear everything that Theo's said to you from the Squeak Jar."

"You'd better go," said Ma. She was standing in the doorway. "Your granny spent all day yesterday persuading the Quorum members to hold another extraordinary meeting."

Bea groaned, and swung her legs out of bed. It felt as though she had been asleep for only five minutes. She felt a twinge of guilt. She had not told anyone that the Squeak Jar had lost its squeak. "I suppose the Pearlseeds will be able to tell just by counting the hairs on my eyebrows, or smelling my socks from afar," she muttered under her breath as she stepped out onto the verandah. She descended the ladder and followed Phoebe, who was already trotting back toward the tree where the Quorum met. "Are you going to wait for me?" called Bea.

"What's keeping you?" said Phoebe. She stopped in

the middle of the path and stood with her hands on her hips.

"I'm just tired," said Bea. "I didn't sleep much."

Phoebe gave her a searching look. "You look like pizza dough," she said. "You look worse than Willow. . . ." She paused, and her jaw dropped. She glanced back over her shoulder to make sure nobody was listening. "Did the Ledbetters get you?" she whispered. "When we were in the library?"

Bea nodded, a lump forming in her throat. "Come on," she said.

They fell into step, walking briskly toward the Quorum. "Are you okay?" said Phoebe. "It must be horrible having that scary old crone in your dreams."

"It wasn't Maize," said Bea. "It was Ike—the one who was following us before."

"Really? You mean she doesn't do it herself?"

"I don't know, but it's Ike who appeared in my dream. Maybe she assigns a different squatter to each person."

"A bit like an internship?" said Phoebe.

Bea laughed. She had not wanted to tell anyone about her dream, but now that she had confided in Phoebe her grim secret seemed a little lighter to carry. "I think I might have gotten rid of him," she said.

Phoebe looked at her doubtfully. "Are you sure?"

"No," said Bea, "but I made him go away just before you woke me up."

"But what about Willow and all the others? I thought it was impossible to get them out once they were in your dreams."

"I got some help from Arkadi this morning," said Bea. "After that I wasn't so afraid."

"So he is the real Arkadi after all?"

"He's not denying it anymore."

"I wondered where you'd gone when I woke up," said Phoebe. "I went looking for you, but then Granny Delphine popped out of that big tree like a squirrel with glasses and yelled at me that I'd find you back at the house." They hurried onward, and as they neared the tree Phoebe said, "Could you talk to Theo while Ike was in your dreams?"

"No," said Bea.

"Still," said Phoebe, "even if Ike comes back, at least you still have the Squeak Jar."

"I have the jar," said Bea, without meeting Phoebe's eye.

# Gifted

"The Quorum has summoned you," said Mr. Morganfield, "because Mrs. Walker tells us that you are in contact with your missing brother. Is this true?"

Bea did not answer him directly. Her eyes were not yet accustomed to the dim light inside the tree trunk, and she was glad she could not look her questioner in the eye. Instead she asked, "Are you going to help us find him?"

"Of course," said Mr. Morganfield. "We'd like to give it the utmost priority."

"Please produce the Squeak Jar," said another man. She could dimly see a bald head with a fringe of hair, and she realized that this must be Mr. Horton, who had lost his niece to the Ledbetters' grim tactics. Eight of the chairs circling the chamber were occupied by clan heads. Only Maize Ledbetter was missing. Granny Delphine herself sat in Maize's chair, and if she was worried about Maize turning up she did not show it.

"I don't have it," said Bea. She could feel the weight of the voiceless Squeak Jar in her backpack.

A woman on the far side of the chamber spoke. "Then the jar in your backpack is just . . . an empty jar?"

Bea had no idea how the woman knew what was in her backpack, but she was familiar enough with the nature of Mumbo Jumbo not to be surprised. "That's right," she said, truthfully enough.

Mr. Morganfield stroked his wispy beard and frowned. "Perhaps you could tell us what your brother has said to you already."

"Not much, to be honest," said Bea. "He's only seven. He said that he's in a place where there are thin wavy trees and there's always a breeze."

"I've already told you all this," said Granny Delphine sharply. "The boy has been missing for three days now, and we were promised help the day before yesterday. . . ." She continued to berate the Quorum, but Bea was no longer listening.

Something had caught her attention from outside the tree. She tuned in to the sounds of the bees, a habit that she found increasingly easy. There it was again, an empty socket of silence in the buzzing pattern, heading swiftly in their direction. It was still a long way off, but it moved faster and straighter than Ike Ledbetter had. Bea pictured Maize's determined stride and knew instinctively that she must be at the center of it.

"I think we should talk about the Ledbetter problem first," Bea said loudly. Granny Delphine stopped in midsentence. All eyes turned to Bea. She met her grandmother's magnified stare for a moment, and could not help thinking that she knew about Ike Ledbetter's invasion of her dreams. She looked away.

"You are a guest of the Quorum, young lady," said Mr. Morganfield frostily, "and you are certainly not qualified to set the agenda." He gave a rather unconvincing smile. "Besides, I think we are all agreed that locating your little brother is the most urgent task that faces us at the moment."

"It's too late for some," muttered Mr. Horton. He said it under his breath, but Bea was a very good listener, and she did not miss much. She stared at the balding man for a moment as the meaning of his statement sank in.

"You want to find him so you can hand him over to

the Ledbetters!" she said, too astonished to be angry.

Mr. Morganfield cleared his throat. "It's the tradition here, young lady—"

"Over my dead body," interrupted Granny Delphine.

"Some have already died," said Mr. Horton, "and more will follow if we keep holding out against those savages."

"Why don't you just lock them up then?" said Phoebe's voice from the window above them. Granny Delphine shot her a look that could have instantly toasted a marshmallow. "Sorry!" said Phoebe, and Bea could hear her slithering quickly down the rough bark outside.

"All of us in Bell Hoot came here to escape brutal persecution," said Mr. Morganfield. "I have already told you how the tradition of fostering helps to maintain peace and stability. We have never had a need for prisons or police forces, nor do we want them. In Bell Hoot we have the power of Mumbo Jumbo to keep us from re-creating the world we have escaped."

Bea was only half listening to Mr. Morganfield's lecture. She could hear the hurrying silence that was Maize getting closer by the minute. There was something else she could faintly detect too. It sounded like a much larger hole in the buzzing pattern of the bees.

It was some distance away in the direction from which Maize was coming. Unlike the silence that surrounded Maize it did not move. Bea frowned as she tried to imagine what it could be.

"If you give in to the Ledbetters you might as well hand Bell Hoot to Maize and go home to your rocking chairs," Granny Delphine was saying.

"It is the Ledbetters' *turn* to foster—," began Mr. Morganfield.

"They don't really want to foster him," interrupted Bea. "Maize Ledbetter has said that the Hidden Boy will be the next head of her clan. That doesn't sound like they'll be giving him back after a year, does it?"

"How did you know about that?" said Mr. Horton. He looked at Bea, then at Granny Delphine.

"Don't look at me," said Granny Delphine. "Even *I* didn't know that."

"It doesn't matter how I know," said Bea. "If you're going to discuss the Ledbetters you'd better do it now. Maize will be here in a few minutes."

Mr. Morganfield cocked his head for a moment. He looked at Granny Delphine and raised his eyebrows. "You've taught her well," he said.

"I haven't taught her anything," said Granny Delphine. "She's gifted."

"There is a way we can beat the Ledbetters," said Bea. "They use people's fear to invade their dreams. All we need to do is figure out what they're afraid of themselves." She wondered what the clan heads would say if they knew that she had brought that idea straight from Arkadi himself.

Mr. Horton laughed bitterly. "The Ledbetters aren't afraid of anything."

"That's where you're wrong," said Bea. She listened to the bees as she spoke, her mind racing. It was still there in the distance, that lake of silence. It conjured up a picture of one of Ma's tattoos. A lake with a bare island. That was it! The beeless silence in the distance must be Mumpfish Lake itself. With no plants or fruit trees left on the island there was no reason for bees to cross such a large expanse of water. The Ledbetters had cut all the trees down—Mr. Miller said so, and Mr. Morganfield himself had confirmed it. She closed her eyes for a moment, and Ma's vividly inked pictures paraded across her mind's eye. Swarming bees, the Ledbetters' barren home, their muffled bodies, herself holding the key. It all began to fall into place. A current of excitement passed through her and she felt breathless, as though she had just run up a flight of stairs. She tried to keep her voice casual. "The Ledbetters *are* afraid of something. They're afraid of bees."

"Bees?" said the woman across the chamber. "Why do you say that, child?"

"They cut down all the fruit trees on their island, didn't they?" said Bea. "No trees, no flowers. No flowers, no bees. And still they live there, even though they can't feed themselves."

"They venture often to the mainland," said Mr. Horton.

"Only when they have to," said Bea. "That's why they're all wrapped up and smelling of camphor—to keep the bees off," she said, as though it were the most obvious thing in the world.

"I told you she was gifted," said Granny Delphine, and Bea could see pride in her eyes.

"What would you suggest doing with this information?" asked Mr. Horton. Some of the bitterness had gone from his voice, and he was watching Bea keenly.

"We need to trick them into giving up invading people's dreams," said Bea. Her mind was racing. Maize Ledbetter would be here any minute, and there was no time for detailed planning. She spoke her thoughts aloud as they came into her head, and hoped that they would make some kind of sense. "We can agree to hand the Hidden Boy over. Then when Maize arrives to take him, I'll use the bees to drive her into the square, and we can make her agree to leave us alone."

"What do you mean, *use* the bees?" said the beefy man who sat next to Mr. Morganfield.

"I can speak to bees, sort of," said Bea. "I think I can make them swarm if I ask them to."

"Sort of?" said the man. "Can you or can't you?"

"If she says she can do it, then she can," said Granny Delphine sharply. "She's been here three days and already she's figured out the Ledbetters' weakness."

Bea tried to look confident. In truth she had no idea whether she would be able to do what she had suggested. She thought about the bees returning obediently to their hive as she had inched down the birch tree two days before. Had they really been responding to her hummed request? It was impossible to be sure. Even if they had been, using them to herd the stubborn Ledbetter clan into a peace agreement might be an altogether different matter. It was a flimsy plan, she knew, but she was fast running out of options.

"It makes no difference whether she can or can't," said Mr. Morganfield. "The Ledbetters won't fall into a trap that easily. Maize wouldn't come to such a meeting alone. She will bring all her sons at least, and they won't come close until they see the Hidden Boy in the flesh."

"They will see him," said Bea. "Only, it won't be him; it will be Phoebe, but they won't know that until it's too late."

"Phoebe?" said the woman across the chamber.

"She's my friend," said Bea. "She has short hair, and we can dress her as a boy. She's small for her age, too. She could easily fool them from a distance, and once they realize their mistake it will be too late."

"So much the better if Maize doesn't come alone, in any case," added Granny Delphine. "If there is any chance to force an agreement from them it will have to include all her sons."

"Maize is approaching," broke in Mr. Morganfield. "It's time for you to leave, Bea."

"I will see the girl out," said Mr. Horton.

Bea climbed down the ladder as quickly as she could. She did not want to be there when Maize Ledbetter arrived, nor was she very comfortable about spending time in Mr. Horton's presence. *Why does he want to see me out?* she wondered. *It's not as if the door is hard to find.*

She reached the bottom of the ladder. Maize Ledbetter was striding purposefully toward her through the ferns. Bea paused, unsure of what to do. She heard Mr. Horton's voice in her ear.

"All trees are thin and wavy, Bea," he whispered. "It just depends on where you're standing." He squeezed Bea's shoulder and gave her a brief smile, as though to apologize for his harsh words earlier.

Bea turned and found herself face-to-face with Maize Ledbetter, who seemed to have covered the last few yards in a flash.

The old woman glared at Bea. "There's scheming afoot," she said in her scratchy crow's voice. "I knows it, an' you know I knows it." She leaned closer, her hot breath smelling of mothballs. "I'll find out what it's all about, and someone will pay dear. You can bet your lights on that, girly." She swept past Mr. Horton without so much as a glance, and disappeared up the ladder into the gloom.

# Perched

"How do I look?" said Phoebe Lu. She was dressed in trousers and a shirt that had been borrowed from one of Mr. Morganfield's grandsons.

"You'll pass for a boy, from a distance," said Granny Delphine.

"Let's hope that's as close as it gets," said Mr. Miller. "I wouldn't like to face Maize Ledbetter when she loses her temper."

"I'm not afraid of her," said Phoebe.

"You should be," said Granny Delphine grimly, "like a kitten should be afraid of a steamroller." She mussed up Phoebe's hair and stepped back to take another look. "Now remember, Morganfield and I will wait with you, but when the Ledbetters are in sight we will have to retreat to the square. That was the agreement, and it was hard enough even to get Maize to that point. You must stand where you are until all the Ledbetters get close enough for Bea to call up her little stripy friends. Once they've surrounded the Ledbetters you'd better turn and run as fast as you can. Are you sure you can do it?"

Phoebe nodded, and Granny Delphine turned to Bea. "You'll be in the big elm tree on the corner of the square. There's a good view right along the path from there. Morganfield says that Mutton Ledbetter always brings up the rear when they're on the move. He's the big one with the limp and the orange whiskers. When you see him coming you'll know they're all there."

The afternoon sun was high above the trees as they made their way toward the town square. The air was drowsy with bees, and Bea listened carefully to locate a hive that was near the path where the handover of the Hidden Boy had been agreed upon. The path led out of the square on the side opposite the library, sloping gently downward until it curved out of sight on its way to Cambio Falls, and beyond the falls to Mumpfish Lake. At the start of the path stood an enormous elm tree whose branches stretched out and shaded almost half the square. Mr. Miller gave Bea a leg up, and she climbed upward until she found a comfortable perch where the smooth trunk forked. A smaller branch extended to her right, and by hooking her arm over it she felt secure enough to look down. She was higher than she expected.

"Can you see along the path?" called Granny Delphine.

"I can see between the leaves," said Bea. "But what happens if they see me?"

"You should be well enough hidden, and once the bees start to swarm, the Ledbetters will have other things to think about," said Granny Delphine. "Until then you'll have to stay as still as possible and hope for the best."

Bea looked down at Phoebe in her Hidden Boy disguise. She did look a little like Theo, if you half closed your eyes. *Besides*, thought Bea, *the Ledbetters can't know what Theo looks like, can they?* She could not help thinking that her plan was far from watertight, but it was essential that it worked. Theo's life probably depended on it. Phoebe's might too. Bea felt dizzy with nervousness. She closed her eyes and gripped the branch beside her for fear she might fall right out of the tree.

"Good luck." Phoebe's voice came from below.

Bea opened her eyes and forced herself to smile. Her throat was dry, so she gave Phoebe a thumbs-up and watched as she set off along the path, flanked by Granny Delphine and Mr. Morganfield. For a while they were lost to view among the leaves, and Bea closed her eyes again to concentrate better on her task.

She had already located a nearby hive, and she tried a little experimental hum to make herself known to the bees. She could hear their pattern change a little, and a couple of drones flew up close to her perch to see what manner of strange bee she was. She knew she would have to make them go around behind the Ledbetters in order to drive them toward the town square, where the other members of the Quorum waited out of sight. It would be a complicated request to make with her very limited grasp of bee language, and she was wondering how she would manage to do it when she became aware of another hive farther along the path.

This hive was a busy one, and from the deep buzz of its occupants she could tell they were fat and numerous. It sounded as if the bees were preparing to swarm, and Bea held her breath while she listened, not daring to believe her good fortune. The hive was just beyond the curve of the path, so that all she needed to do was to persuade them to swarm at the right moment and to head directly for her, driving the Ledbetters before them as they came.

Bea changed the tune of her humming to a lower, honey-laden tone. She could hear a brief drop in the noise of the distant hive as they tried to locate the sound she was making. The bees seemed agitated. Swarming was like an itch they had to scratch, and it created a purposeful racket that sounded so loud to Bea that she wondered how everyone was not deafened by it.

She opened her eyes and looked along the path. Through a gap in the leaves she could see the distant figures of Granny Delphine, Phoebe and Mr. Morganfield. They stood in a row like pins in a bowling alley, waiting for the Ledbetters to roll along the path from the distant lake. A finger of sun found its way down through the canopy and warmed Bea where she perched. She closed her eyes again, listening for the ripples of silence that would signal the approach of the Ledbetters. The drone of the bees stretched into the distance in all directions, and she felt herself suspended in its center, like a drowsy fly in a vast, invisible web. She stifled a yawn. *Wouldn't it be terrible*, she thought to herself, *if I fell asleep right when I'm needed most?*

She blinked and rubbed her eyes. She was sure she had been sitting high in the broad arms of the elm tree, but now she found herself in a small room with blank walls. The room was empty except for a squatting figure with straw-colored hair and washed-out eyes. With a plummeting feeling she realized it was Ike Ledbetter, and before he opened his colorless lips she knew exactly what was coming.

"Give us the Hidden Boy," he said.

# Trigger

**B**ea Flint looked at Ike Ledbetter with a sinking feeling. She knew she had been about to do something very important, but Ike's stare seemed to wash everything useful from her mind. She tried to get a grip on her panic for long enough to make her voice work. "What are you doing here?" she said.

Ike stared dumbly back at her. He seemed a little less certain than before.

"You don't need to do this anymore," persisted Bea. "The Quorum has made an agreement with Maize." She could not remember now exactly what the agreement was, but she knew it was important. Ike said nothing.

"You could be working on your boat," said Bea.

To her surprise a sort of smile broke out on Ike's

face. It was not a face that was used to smiling, and it looked about as comfortable as a left shoe on a right foot.

"Boat's nearly finished," he said. "She'll float true, she will. I makes the best boats." He sat there expectantly.

It was beginning to dawn on Bea why Ike had come back. He wanted to talk. She wondered if anyone had ever tried to be nice to him before. "That sounds . . . um . . . well done," she said.

"I just got to add the rowlocks, and put in a bench."

Bea searched Ike's expression. He did not seem so menacing now, and she almost felt sorry for him. Still, there was a stubborn look on his face, and he seemed as determined as ever to remain where he was. "Why don't you go and do that, then?" said Bea.

Ike shook his head. She waited for an answer, but he said nothing. The anxious feeling increased. She was supposed to be doing something, and it was urgent.

"Why not?" she said.

Ike Ledbetter glanced at his feet. They were grimed with dust, and his toenails were yellow and broken. "Don't want to," he muttered. "I likes it here." He looked up at her and said in a rush, "I'll name the boat for you, only I don't know your name."

"You have to go," said Bea desperately. "I need to . . ." What was it she needed to do? The urgency of her task buzzed at the back of her mind like a bee at a windowpane. "Bees!" she said, suddenly remembering her plan.

"That your name?" said Ike.

"No," snapped Bea. "I mean, yes. It's Bea. Now will you go?"

Ike shook his head again. He had made a friend for the first time in his life. He did not know much about making friends, and even less about keeping them, but it seemed to him that staying put was the best bet.

Bea felt a tightness in her chest. She had left Phoebe out there on her own. The Ledbetters were coming, and timing was everything. She tried to step out of her dream and picture herself perched, sleeping, in the tree, but as long as Ike squatted in her dream she seemed unable to escape it. Her panic turned to anger in an instant. She could neither move nor leave that blank white room, so she did the only other thing she could think of. She began to hum the angry song she had learned from the bees whose honey she had taken.

Ike shrank back against the wall. "What are you

doin'?" he said. "Don't make that noise! You'll wake 'em. You'll wake 'em up."

Bea saw the fear in his eyes. It came from somewhere deeper than his fear of Maize Ledbetter. She hummed on.

"I told you to stop," said Ike. He looked as though he had been slapped in the face. "I thought you was different," he said. "I thought you was nice."

Bea could see Ike's stubbornness increase. He settled in place like a rock, and his face closed down. She hummed louder. A strange tingling ran through her, and she felt something sprouting from her back. It startled her so much that she tried to cry out, but her mouth felt odd and brittle. She could feel herself inflate, and her vision shattered into a million images. At the edges of her kaleidoscopic vision she could see stripes of black and yellow, and her giant furry bee legs planted on the floor below her. *This is not supposed to happen*, she thought to herself. Her enormous wings blew dust around the little room, and her antennae uncurled themselves at the terrified boy in front of her.

Ike was cowering now, his face deathly white beneath the dirt, but the cold malice of his great-grandmother glared out through his saucer eyes.

"That's bad Mumbo Jumbo," he said. "But I'll pay you back. I'll find the Hidden Boy myself. I knows things. I'll find him, and when I get my hands on him you'll be sorry you met me."

In an instant he was gone, leaving nothing but a rapidly fading shadow where he had squatted. Bea tried to close her eyes. The fractured pictures were making her dizzy. "Bees don't have eyelids," she reminded herself. She stopped humming and stilled her wings. She breathed deeply. She blinked. That was a good sign. Her vision slowly returned to normal, and she held her hands out in front of her to make sure she had reverted to her usual self. She felt drained, and for a moment she just sat where she was, staring at the wall opposite. Still her dream showed no sign of dissipating. She scanned the walls for a way out, but the room seemed entirely featureless. She tried to remember everything that Arkadi had told her.

"Everything in this dream is mine," she said aloud. She knew there was no time to lose. "In which case," she added, "I'd like a door."

Before the words were out of her mouth she noticed a hairline crack in the wall in front of her. She was sure it had not been there a moment before. It traced a rectangle that reached almost to head height. "That'll do for a start," said Bea. The feeling that she was back in control ran through her like clear water, and she was on her feet in an instant.

Her legs felt wobbly, as though they were barely strong enough to support her. She went to the door and pushed gently. It swung open without resistance. A green light flooded the room. The rectangle of the door was completely filled with gently fluttering leaves. She reached out for something to hold on to, and a slim branch appeared just where she needed it. A broader one appeared at her feet as she stepped out through the door. *This is not so hard*, she thought. She could see nothing below her but more leaves. Her nostrils were filled with the smell of sap and the fragrance of flowers. She squinted up at the sunlight that filtered through the leaves. High above her the thinner branches swayed in the breeze, and suddenly she remembered the whispered words of Mr. Horton: *All trees are thin and wavy, Bea. It just depends on where you're standing.*

"Of course!" said Bea. She could not imagine why she hadn't thought of it before. "He's up high!" She hesitated for a moment. She knew Phoebe was waiting for her down below, but she was equally sure that

Theo was somewhere above her, and she might never find herself here again. "Theo?" she said. Around her the wind shushed through the leaves like waves on a beach. She called his name again. There was a distant answer, but she could not make out the words. Before she knew what she was doing she was climbing as fast as she could, heading for the sound of Theo's voice. Her legs still felt like jelly, but she set her jaw and kept pushing upward. She reached a layer of thick foliage and intertwined branches that was so dense she had to force her way through it. The branches scratched her skin and she was almost blinded by the light. Here under the sky the trunks were slim and the leaves danced in the breeze. She had never smelled air so fresh.

"Theo?" she called again, squinting against the light.

"Where have you been?" said Theo. "You were gone *forever* this time."

She turned and saw him, sitting on a branch and swinging his legs impatiently. There were twigs in his hair and his eyes were wide with excitement.

"Did you bring Nails with you?" he asked.

Bea shook her head. She had never been so happy to see anyone in her life. Tears welled up in her eyes and she felt as though she would choke. "He's down below," she said. Theo was smiling from ear to ear. His face was about as dirty as it was possible for a small face to be, and there were large ragged holes in the knees of his trousers. She cleared her throat. "Come on; we have to go."

She reached out her hand to Theo, and he jumped down from the branch. She almost expected him to plummet through the leaves, and her heart missed a beat. Instead he bounced toward her across the thick carpet of foliage as though it were the most natural thing in the world. Bea folded him in a big hug.

He squeezed her back with all his might for a second; then he struggled free. "That's enough," he said. "Are we going back to the bus now?"

"No, but we have to go down quickly," said Bea. "Phoebe's in trouble."

"Okay," said Theo; then he hesitated. "I have to say good-bye to the Tree People."

"Where are they?" asked Bea. She looked around her and suddenly realized that they were surrounded by thin figures, watching them from among the swaying branches. She could see them from the corners of her eyes, but when she tried to look straight at them she could see only the trees themselves.

The Tree People were speaking to her. It was as though the wind in the leaves were shaping itself into words. *"You have come to take the Barkless Boy?"* they asked her.

"He's my little brother," said Bea.

*"It's about time,"* said the Tree People. *"We have filled his head up with seeds. If we give him any more he might pop like a ripe fruit."*

"Don't you need to . . . let him go, or something?" asked Bea. Whoever these people were, they had been keeping Theo in a dream. If he just climbed down with her now, would he still be with her when she woke up?

*"You will enter the other world when you go downward,"* said the Tree People. *"The Barkless Boy will return where he belongs. Tonight there will be honey in the bowl."*

Theo looked at Bea and made a quizzical face. "They're always talking like that," he said in a whisper so loud that all of the Tree People for miles around must have heard him. "I haven't a clue what they're on about half the time."

Bea shaded her eyes with her hand to take a last look around. She wished she could see the strange figures properly. They were camouflaged like lizards against the branches. Her eyes were becoming used to the light now, and just as she was about to begin descending she noticed in the clear blue sky the faintest trace of a full moon. The curve of one side ghosted above the tree-tops, and it was pale yellow in color. "Come on," she said to Theo. "We have to go."

There was a fluttering sound, and a large colorful bird half flew, half fell from a higher branch, land-ing on Theo's shoulder with a thump and almost fall-ing straight off again. It was an ancient parrot with bedraggled plumage and several bald patches. The parrot cocked his head to one side and squinted at Bea through cloudy eyes. "Where the blazes are you, Trig-ger?" said the parrot. It sounded like Bontoc's voice played through a tiny speaker. "Went for a flamin' swim, didn't you?"

"I'm bringing Trigger," said Theo, looking at Bea defiantly, as though he expected an argument.

"Fine," said Bea. "Just come quickly." She began to clamber back down the way she had come. She won-dered why a yellow moon was rising now. Captain Bontoc had said it was not due for three weeks, but the climb needed all of her concentration, and she put the puzzle of the moon to the back of her mind. Now that her eyes were accustomed to the bright light above she could no longer find her footing in the gloom. Her muscles ached and her hands were soon sticky with sap. She looked up to make sure Theo was following her. Her foot slipped and she almost fell. Theo was climbing down carefully, steadying Trigger whenever he had a chance. The ancient parrot seemed in permanent danger of toppling off his shoulder.

The tree seemed to stretch downward forever, its trunk getting thicker all the time. She came to a fork in the trunk and recognized it as the one where she had been perched while she waited for the Ledbetters to arrive. "I must be awake now," she said to herself, "otherwise I'd meet myself sitting here in the fork." She was not sure if this made any sense.

"Who are you talking to?" said Theo, letting himself down beside her.

"Nobody," said Bea. An idea came to her. "Theo, remember I asked you to pinch me and I didn't feel a thing?"

Theo looked at her suspiciously. "Ye-es," he said slowly.

"Do it again," she said, and when Theo hesitated she snapped, "Don't argue!"

Theo reached out and gripped the flesh of her arm in his small white fingers. He stuck his tongue out of the corner of his mouth and twisted with gusto. It was like being savaged by a pair of deranged pliers. Bea bit her lip and her eyes watered. "Thanks," she said.

"Anytime," said Theo.

Bea looked out along the path. The evening sun slanted through the trees, and at first she could see nothing in the shadows between the sunbeams. She listened for the hive that had been preparing to swarm. There was buzzing everywhere, and she noticed for the first time that the elm was flowering. The bees from the nearer hive were working all around her, creating a pattern like a giant fuzzy hairnet around the tree.

As she strained her ears to penetrate the nearby sounds she spotted the lone figure of Phoebe, standing dead still in the dappled shade of the forest path. Mr. Morganfield and Granny Delphine must have retreated to the square already. There was movement among the trees on either side of the path. Pale figures were slipping between the trunks like ghosts. They were moving rapidly toward Phoebe, and had already come closer than they should be. Panic hatched in Bea's stomach. She saw Maize Ledbetter now, approaching

swiftly along the center of the path, muffled up against
the bees. Bea tried to repeat the deeper hum of the bees
that she was relying on to swarm, but in the urgency of
the moment she found it harder than usual to concentrate. She could not hear for sure if she was getting any
reaction from the distant hive.

Theo was looking at her oddly. "What are you humming?" he said.

"Sssh!" said Bea, putting her finger to her lips.

"I learned a wind song from the Tree People," said
Theo. "Do you want to hear it?"

Bea shook her head. The Ledbetters had fanned
out in the woods on either side of Phoebe. They were
moving to cut her off. Fear spread through Bea like ice
water. Maize had come to a halt now, no more than
twenty paces from Phoebe. She was staring at her, but
Bea could not read her expression from such a distance.
She felt her plan rapidly unraveling. "Wait here," she
said urgently to Theo, and she slid from her perch and
began to slither and drop from branch to branch.

"Where are you going?" she heard Theo call.

"Where the blazes are you?" added Trigger in Bontoc's voice.

"Stay put!" she shouted. "I'll come back for you."

Sweat stung her eyes and the bark of the tree scraped her legs and arms raw. She landed badly among the elm's knobbly roots, twisting her ankle. The pain burned like fire. She pulled herself upright, biting hard on her lip.

As she limped around to the path she heard an enraged squawk from the direction of the falls. "Scheming and trickery!" Maize screeched. She raised a quivering arm and pointed, and her eyes burned with a pale malevolence. On either side her sons and her grandsons closed in on Phoebe, whose disguise looked suddenly foolish and transparent. As Bea watched in horror Maize Ledbetter made a twisting motion with her outstretched hand, and Phoebe dropped instantly to the ground, as though her very soul had been jerked from her body.

# Swarm

**B**ea Flint stood on her one good leg, her hand on the rough bark for support and her twisted ankle throbbing with pain. She had awoken from a dream to find herself in a nightmare. The ancient trees leaned in over the path, holding at bay the last of the evening light, and in the cobwebbed darkness she could see the Ledbetters clustering around the lifeless figure of Phoebe. Mutton Ledbetter, a big lumbering man with a limp, hoisted her onto his shoulder like a half-empty sack of feathers.

Maize Ledbetter stood where she was, her arm still extended. She turned slightly like a squat weather vane and pointed directly at Bea. Her scratchy voice carried along the twilit path. "This one goes in the lake," she croaked. "She'll fatten up the fishes nicely, I reckon. We don't eat children, despite what your friends might say, but we is partial to a nice bit o' fish. We'll be coming back for you, girly, when it gets good and dark."

Bea was frozen to the spot. It was like being in that tiny room with Ike Ledbetter, but she was not dreaming now. She glanced over her shoulder. In the shadows at the edge of the square she could just see the members of the Quorum. Granny Delphine was there, and Morganfield, who could hear for miles, and Horton, who had lost his niece. They were muttering urgently among themselves, and she knew they must be well aware of what was happening. She felt a fool. Her beginner's grasp of Mumbo Jumbo had made her so cocky that she had taken on the entire Quorum and promised them she could take on the Ledbetters too. She had let Granny Delphine down, and put Phoebe in mortal danger. She knew that in a moment the Quorum would reach a decision. They would have to act to save Phoebe, and she would forever be the child who made such a mess of things that Bell Hoot's pacifist ways, already tarnished by the Ledbetters, were lost for good.

She felt a flash of anger melting through her fear. She turned to see the Ledbetters trotting swiftly away toward the lake, carrying Phoebe with them. She did not know if her friend was alive or dead. "Girly, is it?" she said, and she began to hum. It was a loud and urgent hum. A tremendous cloud of sound broke out in response from the distant hive at the curve of the path. The hive was packed to bursting with fat, restless bees. They were fueled up with nectar and waiting for the starting gun. Bea focused on their song, shutting out every other sound. She closed her eyes and burrowed into the center of the hive until she heard the old queen's buzz. She took the sound and made it her own.

MMMMMMMMMMMMMMMMMMMM, she buzzed, and all at once the fat bees burst from their hive like a million miniature helicopters. Bea opened her eyes. The Ledbetters had stopped in their tracks at the curve of the path. Around them the air was thickening by the second. A dense swarm of black dots fizzed against the yellow backdrop of the moon that sat like a full bowl of honey on the horizon.

Bea called to the swarm. She ordered them to fly low and to make their way toward her. The bees were elated to be free from the hive, and ready to do anything she asked. They formed a fuzzy cordon around the Ledbetters, who spun around in terror, looking for a way out. Some flapped their arms and yelled in panic, while others covered their heads and crouched low. Mutton dropped Phoebe to the ground and pulled his ragged scarf up around his ears.

The bees began to move, and Maize, who had been at the head of the column, turned back toward Bea with a cry of rage. She began to drive her clan ahead of her like an agitated sheepdog, aiming a kick here and a box there to keep them moving smartly. Bea watched, transfixed, as they tripped and fell and rolled upright again, no less afraid of Maize's wrath than of the bees themselves. The roar of wings grew louder by the second.

Bea hopped gingerly back off the path as the swarm drew near, blowing dust and dry leaves before it like a small hurricane. In its center the Ledbetters were fearful and confused, but not Maize. She was marching toward the square now with grim determination in her eyes. As she drew level with Bea the old woman suddenly lunged in her direction, breaking through the swarm. Bea stumbled backward. Her twisted ankle gave way and she fell to the packed earth. A layer of angry bees coated the old woman, and Bea stared in dismay as they began to sting her mercilessly.

*Enough!* Bea hummed, as loudly as she could. *Leave her alone.* The noise was so loud she did not know if the bees would hear her. *Up!* she commanded. *Fly up!* It was the only thing she could think of. The bees began to lift off from Maize. They were joined by the others in the swarm, and within moments a funnel of bees was rising into the air as though they were being sucked up by the moon.

Maize Ledbetter dropped to her knees. Her yellowish skin was turning an angry red, and she was swelling up like a grub.

Bea struggled to her feet. The Ledbetters stood in a sullen knot where their buzzing herders had deserted them. "Help her!" shouted Bea, but they just stared at her with dull resentment, as though they had been expecting this all along.

She could see Granny Delphine and Mr. Morganfield hurrying toward her across the square.

The rapidly ballooning Maize seemed to be trying to speak. Bea leaned closer in horrified fascination. Maize's words squeaked out through swollen lips. "Must be my birthday," she said. "I knowed for many years I would die this day." She paused for a moment, gasping for breath. "I knowed it was bees that would do me in, too," she wheezed. "Only way to bring out the . . . Hidden Boy, as it turns out. It's all got to work together. Didn't . . . see that bit till now."

"What can I do?" asked Bea.

"Can't do nothing, girly. Just step aside." She waved a bloated hand that looked like an inflated rubber glove. Bea hopped to one side, puzzled. Maize was staring at someone beyond her. "Your turn now, boy," she said. "You is head of the Ledbetter clan. Don't roll over for nobody."

Bea spun around, following Maize Ledbetter's gaze. Theo stood there among the roots, a bedraggled parrot on his shoulder and his jaw hanging open in amazement at the sight of the pink swollen woman kneeling before him.

"It's your fate, boy," squeaked Maize. "Can't escape it, neither. Even old Ma Ledbetter can't escape her fate." She gave a jerky wheeze that sounded almost like a laugh; then she toppled slowly over and was still.

# Head

A fat yellow moon hung over the main square of Bell Hoot. It looked as though a circular hole had been cut in the evening sky to let some daylight through. Half the population of the town had converged on the main square as news had spread of Maize Ledbetter's death and the return of the Hidden Boy. Ma was there, sitting on the steps of the library, her arms wrapped so tightly around Theo that it looked as if she would never let him go. Theo in turn hugged Nails the meerkat, and both boy and meerkat had given up struggling and submitted to their fate. Clockwork Gabby sat beside them, straight as a pencil, a wide smile bisecting her face, and Trigger the parrot, ousted from his perch on Theo's shoulder, stalked up and down the steps and sulked. "Where the blazes are you, Trigger?" he muttered from time to time.

Pa had given Theo such a mighty bear hug that Ma had had to send him off to rescue Phoebe from where she lay, for fear that he might squeeze the boy to death. As he thundered along the path Pa wiped tears from his eyes with the backs of his tattooed hands. He hoped that nobody would notice, then realized that he really didn't care if they did.

A knot of some twenty Ledbetters squatted sullenly in the middle of the square. The library had been unlocked and a desk carried out and set in front of them, along with three chairs on which sat Mr. Morganfield, Mr. Horton and Granny Delphine. Mr. Morganfield was clearing his throat and tapping a pencil on the table, but nobody paid him much attention.

The ballooned body of Maize Ledbetter had been covered by the largest sheet that could be found, and lighted candles had been placed at her head, hands and feet to light her way home, as was the custom in Bell Hoot.

Bea had sent the bees on their way, and was waiting anxiously for Pa to return with Phoebe. As they came into view she gave a huge sigh of relief to see that Phoebe was walking, albeit somewhat shakily, on her own two feet. She was holding on to Pa's arm for support.

Mr. Morganfield cleared his throat more loudly, and the babble of the assembled crowd subsided. Two yellow moons in less than a week, strange tales of swarming bees and the death of Bell Hoot's most feared matriarch had given them plenty to talk about, but they could see there was more to come.

"The Quorum of Bell Hoot is now in session," said Mr. Morganfield, "and let us hope this will be the last extraordinary session for some time." He shuffled some papers on the desk. The papers were advertisements for yoga classes, book clubs and missing cats that Miss Hopkins had been sorting for the library notice board, but for people who regularly preside over meetings paper shuffling is a hard habit to break.

"The Quorum would like to extend its sympathies to the entire Ledbetter family on their tragic loss," began Mr. Morganfield. Mr. Horton examined his fingernails and frowned. "However," Mr. Morganfield continued, "the passing of Maize Ledbetter presents an excellent opportunity to turn over a new leaf."

"Glad to hear it," said Mutton Ledbetter.

"I was referring to you, Mr. Ledbetter," said Mr. Morganfield. "As the senior member of your clan I assume you will take over as leader. The Quorum demands that you cease harassing the citizens of Bell Hoot, and leave at once the dreams of all those whom you have afflicted to date."

Mutton Ledbetter shrugged. "No need for that no more. The Hidden Boy is found. He's the new head of the Ledbetters. You'd best talk with him."

"Don't be ridiculous," said the beefy man, who stood with his arms folded behind Mr. Morganfield. "The boy is only six or seven, and he's not even of your clan."

"Each clan got the right to choose their own leader," said Mutton. "That's Bell Hoot law, and you been spouting the law at us since as long as I can remember, Morganfield. Old Ma told us over and over the Hidden Boy'd be the next leader. Said she'd live to a hundred too, and not a day more, and there she is lying dead on her hundredth birthday. Everything she ever said come true, and this won't be no different. Can't nobody escape their fate."

"Who's the Hidden Boy?" said Theo. He had finally allowed Nails to escape from his arms, and the meerkat had settled beside him on the library step, his head on

Theo's lap and his little snout sniffing for beetles in his master's pocket.

The Ledbetters turned as one to look at Theo. "You is," said Mutton.

Theo's eyes opened wide. "You want *me* to be your leader?" he said incredulously.

Ma tightened her hold on Theo. "You must be joking!" she said. "I won't be letting Theo out of my sight, not for a second. It's an absurd suggestion any-way—he's just a baby."

"No, I'm not," said Theo indignantly. He turned to Mutton Ledbetter. "We're only here on holiday, though."

Mutton Ledbetter laughed. "That's what they told you, maybe. There's no way back from Bell Hoot, boy. You're here for good."

Theo looked at Ma, but she was avoiding his eye. He turned to Bea. "Are we really?" he said. Bea nodded.

Mr. Horton looked up from his fingernails and fixed Mutton Ledbetter with a cold stare. "If you knew all along that the Hidden Boy would be found," he said, "why was it necessary to bully all those people with your insidious tricks? Why did my sister's child have to die?"

"Maize didn't mean for no one to die. She just wanted

the boy sooner, is all," said Mutton. "She knowed her time was running out. She wanted to teach the boy our ways before she up and died, didn't she? You should have handed him over."

"We couldn't have done so even if we had wanted to," said Granny Delphine "We arrived only three days ago, and he's been lost since then." She was interrupted by a piercing screech from the bedraggled parrot on the library steps. Trigger made a short run and took off, skimming the heads of the assembled Ledbetters and almost colliding with Mr. Horton, who ducked just in time to avoid getting a faceful of ancient parrot.

There was an astonished cry from the far side of the square. It was Captain Bontoc. He had just walked from Cambio Falls, his head abuzz with strange events, and the last thing he had expected was to find his long-lost parrot heading for him like a flying feather duster. "Trigger!" he cried.

"Where the blazes are you, Trigger?" said the parrot happily. He tried to land on the captain's shoulder, but his momentum was too great and his brakes had long since ceased to work. He glanced off Bontoc's ear and fluttered to rest on the sheet-covered mound that was the mortal remains of Maize Ledbetter.

Captain Bontoc was so overjoyed to see the parrot that he did not seem to notice the grim nature of his perch. He lifted Trigger and placed him gently on his shoulder.

Mr. Morganfield looked up pointedly at the moon. A blue cast was spreading across it, chasing the yellow back into hiding. "Bontoc!" he said sharply. "The crossing, man! What about the numbers?"

"Crossing has been made, Morganfield," said Bontoc. He scratched his head in a puzzled fashion, and Bea noticed he wasn't wearing his cap. It was the first time she had ever seen him without it.

"What do you mean?" demanded Morganfield. "Nine souls must go through. You know that."

"No one knows better," agreed Bontoc. "Funny thing happened tonight, though. Firstly it wasn't supposed to be no yellow moon. Chart said the next one is in three weeks; I'm sure of it."

"You must have read it wrong," said Mr. Horton.

"You can check it yourself," said Captain Bontoc cheerfully. "Anyhow, it so happened I was on the Blue Moon Mobile fixing the periscope, which has been jamming lately, when I noticed the yellow moon rising. Naturally I took out my keys, but that was as far as I got." He paused, and his pink cheeks turned slightly pinker.

"Well?" said Granny Delphine. "Are you going to tell us what happened or just stand there blushing like a schoolgirl?"

"You won't believe this," said Bontoc, "but before I could get into the driver's seat who should step aboard but Arkadi himself!"

There was an intake of breath from the entire crowd. Even the Ledbetters looked astonished. Bontoc realized they were hanging on his every word, and he dragged out his pause for dramatic effect. "He took the keys from my hand, cool as you like," he said finally. "Took my cap too. 'Take the night off, Bontoc,' he said, and he sat down in the driver's seat and started the engine."

"That's impossible!" said Mr. Morganfield. "Arkadi has been dead for forty years."

"He's been missing for forty years," Bontoc corrected him, "but it was him nonetheless. I'd stake my life on it. Met him once before when I was a lad, and I'll never forget those eyes. Looked right through me and out the back of my head."

Bea exchanged glances with Phoebe, who sat on the step beside her now, sipping a warm drink that Mrs.

Miller had brought for her. She was still pale, but she gave a little smile.

"Anyhow, I got off the bus like I was told, and Arkadi made the crossing instead," said Captain Bontoc. "Going to make a right mess of the schedule when Cap'n Fuller gets here."

"Are we all done with the chitchat?" interrupted Mutton Ledbetter loudly. "Only we'd like to take the boy and be gettin' back home. We got an old lady to bury."

"You're not taking him anywhere," said Ma fiercely.

"Sit down, please, Captain Bontoc," said Mr. Morganfield. He turned back to face Mutton. "We are not finished, Mr. Ledbetter. The Quorum proposes that your compound on Mumpfish Island be dismantled, and that your clan come to live here in Bell Hoot, where you can be better integrated into the community."

A mutter of discontent rippled through the crowd. It was the first they had heard of this idea, and it was clear that not everyone liked it. The Ledbetters looked angry too.

"You can't throw us off the island," said Mutton. "That's been our home for always. I built half that compound with my own hands."

"You live on a *real* island?" said Theo.

"All our lives," said Mutton.

Theo looked up at Ma. "Where are we going to live?" he said.

"We're staying with some nice people at the moment," said Ma. "We'll have to see what happens later."

"You always say that," said Theo. He turned back to Mutton. "Do you have to do everything your leader says?"

"Always did what Maize told us," said Mutton.

"Even if she told you to wear a pink dress, you'd have to do it?"

"Maize weren't the pink-dress type," said Mutton.

Bea could see the cogs turning in Theo's mind, and she knew what was coming.

"Just suppose I did become the leader," said Theo slowly, "and I told you to build a house for my whole family on the island, would you have to do it?"

Mutton nodded. "If we gets to stay on the island, I reckon that's a fair swap," he said.

Theo looked at Ma. She shook her head. "I don't think that's a good idea," she said.

"I think Theo is right," said Bea.

"Theo is not right," said Ma sharply. "I'm still head of this family, and I say where we live and what happens to us."

Pa opened his mouth to speak, then thought better of it and closed it again.

Ma turned to Mr. Morganfield. "The Quorum will have to provide us with a house. We were brought here under false pretenses, and since you seem to be the nearest thing to a government it's your responsibility to house us."

"We got the right to choose our leader," repeated Mutton. Bea could see on his face the same stubborn look she knew from Ike.

Mr. Morganfield sighed. "That is the law," he conceded.

Bea looked at Ma. "It makes sense, Ma," she said. "We need somewhere to live. If Theo becomes head of the clan he can insist they plant the island again. Imagine the whole island covered in fruit trees! I could keep bees, and we could sell the fruit and honey at the market. You could take up tattooing again, if there's anyone left to tattoo."

"No bees!" said the Ledbetters with one voice.

"You don't have to be afraid of bees anymore," said

Bea. "Maize knew that bees would be the end of her. No wonder she was always afraid of them. Bees won't hurt you if you leave them alone. I'll make sure of that."

"Wait a minute," said Theo. "Are meerkats allowed on the island?"

"We got dogs, chickens, plenty of fleas," said Mutton, counting off the species on his fingers. "Don't suppose meerkats lay eggs, do they?"

"Of course not," said Theo. "Anyway, Nails is a boy." He raised his eyes to the fat blue moon. "I can see I'll have my work cut out here," he said under his breath, but only Bea and Mr. Morganfield heard him.

# Question

A bumblebee flew across a calm stretch of water. He flew straight as an arrow, his fat furry reflection keeping pace in the rippled mirror of the lake. He came from a hive newly established by the lakeshore, and he was headed for the sweet heather flowers that the hive's scouts had found on the island at the lake's center.

The heather had been carefully transplanted by Bea and Phoebe from a hillside to the south of the lake, and it had taken root quickly in the scrubby soil of the island. Ike Ledbetter had helped them with the planting. When Bea had first moved to the island he had done his best to ignore her, but he found the business of maintaining a lifelong grudge surprisingly tiring, and on the whole he found being in her company far more enjoyable than sulking in his boat. Neither of them ever mentioned the giant bee incident.

Around the Ledbetter compound a new orchard was taking shape. It was planted with saplings that had been donated by the citizens of Bell Hoot from their own nurseries. It was Granny Delphine's idea to ask for contributions of young trees rather than seeds, so that the Ledbetters' new orchard could begin to produce all the sooner. The fruit growers had responded promptly and generously, though Bea was wise enough to understand that they would also be relieved to see the Ledbetters able to support themselves once again without resorting to burglary.

On this particular day a barbecue was being held to celebrate the completion of the new house. It was a handsome and sturdy house, built by Mutton Ledbetter and his brothers with timber cut from the forest and poled across the lake in makeshift rafts. It stood on a rise a little way off from the main compound, and although it would be occupied by Ma, Pa, Granny Delphine, Theo, Bea, Phoebe and Clockwork Gabby it had already become known as Master Theo's house, a title that seemed likely to stick.

Bea was showing the Millers the place where she planned to build her hives, on a gentle slope on the sunny side of the house. "Once the fruit trees have settled in and the heather has spread there should be enough flowers for a dozen hives to begin with," she said. She had borrowed every book on beekeeping that the Bell Hoot Library contained, but to build the hives she needed Ike's skill with wood. He was still very wary of bees, but she had shown him the hive designs in the borrowed books; and as she had hoped, his enthusiasm for woodworking had overcome his fears, and he had already begun to search for suitable timber.

"How will you get the bees to come and live in the hives?" asked Willow.

Bea smiled at her. The Willow who had asked the question was a lively and elegant girl with a contagious chuckle, almost unrecognizable from the whey-faced ghost who had drifted around the Millers' balcony only months before. "You have to capture a queen," said Bea, "and the rest will follow."

Willow's eyes widened. "Can I help," she asked, "when the time comes?"

"Of course," said Bea.

"If Big Chief Theo allows it," added Phoebe under her breath.

Most of the Ledbetter clan had accepted Maize's

word that Theo should be their new head, and they had ratified her choice by electing him leader under the laws of Bell Hoot. In practical terms it was Mutton Ledbetter who took care of the day-to-day running of the clan, but he always cleared major decisions with Theo first.

For his own part Theo had reluctantly abandoned his idea of making Mutton wear a pink dress to test the power of his new position, and instead had issued some rules that showed a wisdom greater than most seven-year-old boys possess. He ruled that no member of the clan should steal from or harass any citizen of Bell Hoot, and that where possible they should repay in goods or labor what they had stolen in the past.

On hearing of Tilly Horton's tragic death he had ordered the Ledbetters to build a playground in the center of Bell Hoot before even a plank of his own family's house was put in place. With the approval of the Quorum he named it Tilly's Garden, and it took shape and bloomed under the direction of Martha and Coco Ledbetter, two of Ike's aunts whose natural talent for gardening had been of little use to them under Maize's rule. There were slides and swings, tree houses and hidden corners, and it quickly became a favorite place for the children of Bell Hoot, Tilly's younger brothers and sisters among them.

There were some members of the Ledbetter clan who had not been able to settle so easily into this new way of living. The occasional burglary still occurred in Bell Hoot, and the livestock that began to repopulate Mumpfish Island contained a few more sheep and pigs than had been willingly donated by the mainland farmers. Then there was Silver Ledbetter, Maize's only daughter and a hard-faced replica of her mother, who had announced that no stranger's pup would ever be telling *her* what to do, before disappearing into the woods on the day of Maize's funeral. She was followed soon afterward by her sly younger brother Yoric, and no trace had been seen of either of them since.

By and large, however, the clan had settled well enough under Theo's and Mutton's leadership. They were soon feeling the benefits of working for themselves instead of laboring for others, and a wary trust had grown between the townspeople of Bell Hoot and those Ledbetters who began to bring their surplus produce to market.

They had accepted Clockwork Gabby too, without seeming to notice her strangeness. There was no

shortage of hands to wind her key when she began
to slow down, and in any case Bea was almost sure
she had begun to last a day or two without needing
to be wound at all. Gabby still made careful notes in
the small green notebook that she carried with her,
though no one was allowed to see what she was writing. She spoke rarely, as though words were scarce and
might run out at any moment, but she worked hard
and smiled more frequently than she ever had before.

And so they sat around on benches and logs on that
warm summer evening, as the sun neared the horizon and the visiting bees started their return journey
across the lake. There was Granny Delphine and Pa
and the No Longer Hidden Boy, the tattoo artist, her
bee-charming daughter and her daughter's best friend.
There was the half-tamed Ledbetter clan; Captain
Bontoc and his counterpart, Captain Fuller—who
were still trying to figure out how they would restore
balance to the captains' roster; the Hortons, who
had lost a daughter; and the Millers, who had gotten
theirs back; the clan heads and the farmers; the crafts-
people and the librarian and the clockwork lady with
the invisible key. They sipped Gladys Miller's plumegranate juice and wine from Horton's vineyard, and

picked roast pork from between their teeth as the conversation drifted through the company like the smoke
from the slowly cooling embers.

"He wouldn't have been gone that long without
a very good reason," Captain Bontoc was saying,
returning to the well-worn topic of Arkadi's surprise
reappearance.

"It beats me how he could have stayed hidden all
those years, whatever his skills," said Mr. Miller. "It's
not as though Bell Hoot is such a big place."

"He may not have been in Bell Hoot all that time,"
said his wife.

"Where else could he have been?" said Bontoc.
"There's only one way in and out, and every soul is
accounted for on the crossing."

Bea glanced at Phoebe, who winked back at her.
She looked quickly at Granny Delphine, and was not
altogether surprised to receive a knowing look through
her grandmother's singular spectacles.

"If you ask me," said Captain Fuller, "he was an
unwilling guest of the Gummint all that time. Only
reason—"

He was interrupted by Bontoc, who cleared his
throat loudly and nodded in the direction of Clockwork

Gabby. She seemed to be busy scraping leftovers from plates for the Ledbetters' dogs, but Captain Fuller lowered his voice anyway.

"Only reason I can see that he'd be gone for that long, and not get in touch with anyone."

Bea remembered what Arkadi had said to her about being unavoidably detained. She wondered why the two captains were wary of discussing the Gummint in front of Gabby. Surely they couldn't suspect *her* of being connected to the Gummint! Maybe it was just the reverse, thought Bea with a chill. Bontoc had said that the Gummint carried out experiments on their prisoners, that night on the Millers' balcony. Could that have been what had turned Gabby so strange in the first place?

"It's only a matter of time before they rumble this place," Captain Fuller was saying, lowering his voice still further.

Captain Bontoc guffawed. "Never happen!" he said, giving his gloomy counterpart a hearty slap on the back. "There's only one way in here, and those clowns would never figure it out, not if it had a big neon sign on it."

"It has," said Bea.

"You're not wrong, Miss Flint," agreed Bontoc, "but it says 'Mr. Waxy,' not 'This Way to the Hidden Bolt-hole of Bell Hoot.' Gummint men come in there all the time to get their little cars polished. Long as old Waxy don't press the wrong button they'll never be any the wiser." He chortled at the thought, but Bea noticed that Captain Fuller did not seem amused.

On the far side of the fire Theo was describing to a captive audience what it felt like to implode on an underwater bus.

"It was like falling asleep and turning inside out at the same time in a huge bucket of marshmallows with a choir singing backward and fireworks going off and your mouth full of lizards," he said. He waited for that description to sink in, then added thoughtfully: "Only not really like that."

Bea smiled to herself. She had heard Theo describe his strange experience several times before, and each time the description was different. As always she was relieved to hear that he made no mention of the Tree People. She had repeated to him Arkadi's suggestion that he should not speak of them, but it seemed to her that he had half forgotten them anyway, as though they had wiped themselves gently from his memory, in the same way their own memories were cleared at the dawn of each new day.

"But what kind of place were you in, when everyone was searching for you?" asked Willow.

"Bea knows," said Theo vaguely.

"Beanos," echoed Clockwork Gabby, and suddenly a light came on in Bea's head.

Phoebe leaned over toward her. "So *that's* what she meant," she whispered.

Bea nodded. "She must have known all along that I'd find the answer."

"The answer to what?" asked Phoebe.

Bea felt the last of the sun on her face and closed her eyes, half conscious of the distant murmur of the bees as they changed sentries and stocked their honeycombs on the lakeshore. She smiled. "Arkadi would probably say that that's the right question," she said.